Charles Nordhoff

Cape Cod and All Along Shore

Stories

Charles Nordhoff

Cape Cod and All Along Shore
Stories

ISBN/EAN: 9783744748377

Printed in Europe, USA, Canada, Australia, Japan

Cover: Foto ©Andreas Hilbeck / pixelio.de

More available books at **www.hansebooks.com**

ALL ALONG SHORE:

Stories.

By CHARLES NORDHOFF.

„Man hat keine Palmen und Kameele nöthig um Gut zu sein; und Gutsein ist besser als Schönheit."—Heinrich Heine.

NEW YORK:

HARPER & BROTHERS, PUBLISHERS,

FRANKLIN SQUARE.

1868.

TO THE STUPID READER.

THE stories collected in this volume have been printed at different times in *Harper's Magazine*, except one which appeared in the *Atlantic Monthly*. Collections of stories like this, I have noticed, are commonly published at the earnest solicitation of friends, or to gratify the desires of an amiable but undiscriminating public. To prevent misunderstanding in the present case, it is perhaps well to say that the public is guiltless in respect to this volume, and that no fond friend has ever expressed even a willingness to have my stories assume this more enduring form—except the publishers, who, it will be readily believed, have no especial desire to see the book permanently on their shelves.

I have noticed that it is customary with writers, when they collect their shorter tales, to set them into one general story, which serves as a frame-work to the small pieces, and furnishes a name for the volume, such as the "Queen of Hearts" of Mr. Wilkie Collins, and Miss Edwards's "Miss Carew." In this way a story writer gives his collection the appearance, at first sight, of what is called a novel. It naturally occurred to me to follow this fashion, which has the advantage of deceiving purchasers, who buy what they imagine from the title and chapter heads to be a novel, and do not discover, until they get home, that what they took to be a fat chicken is only a small basket full of stale eggs. But I refrained, for two reasons: 1st., I think it wrong to practice such a cheat upon an unoffending and confiding public; and, 2dly., I tried in vain to invent a tale which should serve me as such a frame-work; and had at last to give it up, for lack of ingenuity.

CONTENTS.

CAPTAIN TOM: A RESURRECTION...................................... 13

WHAT IS BEST?.. 47

A STRUGGLE FOR LIFE... 95

ELKANAH BREWSTER'S TEMPTATION................................ 119

ONE PAIR OF BLUE EYES... 151

MEHETABEL ROGERS'S CRANBERRY SWAMP....................... 173

MAUD ELBERT'S LOVE MATCH...................................... 215

CAPTAIN TOM: A RESURRECTION.

CAPTAIN TOM: A RESURRECTION.

IN one of his letters to Coleridge, Charles Lamb raises the interesting question, "Whether an immortal and amenable soul may not come to be damned at last, and the man never suspect it beforehand?" Which starts in a thoughtful mind the further query : "How long could a man live after he was thus dead and damned?"

To the latter question, I suppose that only a proximately correct answer could be given, viz.: It depends: First, upon what manner of soul the dead man has; and, secondly, perhaps, upon what manner of body he has.

That there are men thus insensibly dead I consider beyond a doubt. I meet such frequently in Broadway and Wall Street in which last place they exhibit a degree of movement which is horrid enough to me who know their case; and to convince the skeptical reader, I propose to relate here some singular circumstances in the life of one of these Dead Men, who—to set the matter beyond a doubt—has but lately suffered a resurrection: for how could there be a resurrection if death had not foregone?

When Tom Baker had attained the mature age of ten
years he began to strike out for himself. This was necessary, because Tom's father, who should have struck out
for him, was dead. Uncle Amaziah Baker was a man
who had all his life "sailed very near the wind," as they
say on the Cape of one who finds his expenses threatening continually to exceed his income; and who, in consequence, affects patched trowsers, darned socks, second-
hand fish-boots, and a hat which was in fashion a good
many years ago, namely, when he was married. The
fact is, Uncle Amaziah was an unlucky man; and to be
a fisherman and unlucky: surely nothing could be unluckier than that.

Uncle Amaziah had what is facetiously, but unfeeling-
ly, called a large wife and several small children. The
large wife was a blessing to him; for she helped the income more than she did the outlay, being not only large
but healthy, smart, frugal, and a scold. The children
were—well, the children were put to bed at seven o'clock,
to be out of the way, and blessed their stars when they
got their little stomachs full without a scolding.

Uncle Amaziah, as I have already said, was notoriously
unlucky. In his youth he had tried hard to be a smart
fisherman. He was to have a vessel when he was twenty-
two, and on the strength of that prospect fell desperately
in love with Prudence Robbins, who didn't love him in
return, and told him so at his special request. Whereupon Amaziah turned about and offered his wounded
heart and prospective fishing-schooner to Elmira Rogers;
and she, having sometime before experienced a hankering

after him, incontinently took him up—which, being a large woman while he was a smallish man, she was well able to do.

When Amaziah got his schooner Elmira got her Amaziah. Whether he came to her with a whole heart is more than I can tell. He had a whole coat, and a whole week's holiday, and then went to live at his father-in-law's, who liked his son-in-law so well that he presently built him a small house a mile off, into which the young couple moved when Captain Amaziah came home for the winter.

I am afraid I shall again have to state the fact that Captain Amaziah Baker was an unlucky man. He had a new vessel, he had a new crew, he had brand spanking new fish-gear; but he had his old luck. When the first-fare men came in from the Banks, he was at the tail of the heap; and he spent so much time in washing out his fish, and bewailing his ill-luck, careening his vessel and proving that Heaven had a spite against him, that the owners lost all patience with him, and all hope of their second fare: in which last they were not disappointed; for he came back from the Banks on Thanksgiving Day, and hadn't wet his salt! However, as he himself remarked to an irate shoresman: "We'm not so bad off arter all; got more fish than Jonathan Young, 'nd there ain't no sharper feller 'n he on the Cape."

Now, when you hear an unlucky fisherman comforting himself at the expense of an unluckier, you may guess that his jig's up.

" 'Tain't whistlin' makes the plow go," said Uncle Shu-

bael, from whom I had these preliminary facts; "Captain
Amaziah was willin' enough; but wishers 'nd woulders
makes poor housekeepers, 'nd sayin' 'nd doin's two things.
Ef young men mean to git along these days, they must
fly 'round, 'n' study 'n' *du* all in one breath. It's all very
fine fur the captain to work hard, but airly up may be
never the nearer, 'nd forecast's better'n work-hard any
day; 'n' thet's what Amaziah never hed. But ye can't
make a fog-horn out of a pig's tail; the squeal ain't in
that end, ye know. He allers *wus* right down *on*lucky,
'nd as my old gran'ther used to say, them thet's born under a three ha'penny star 'll never be wurth two-pence.
He warn't jest slow, but he couldn't never strike when
the iron was het. When *he* sailed other folks fished, 'nd
when he hove to the fish was always gone. He usen't
to keep with the fleet, 'nd thet's a sign o' conceit in a
young man. When he lost he al'ays put on a smooth
face, 'n' said 'good enough;' but good enough's a poor
shoat, 'n' though good's good, better's better, *I* think.
'Tain't a good sign when a young feller gits so's't he kin
stan' it to be tail o' the heap; 'nd no wonder Amaziah
stuck there; fur though a man's friends may help along
fur a while, every herrin's got to hang to his own gills:
so what's the use? Them thet's got shall hev, the Bible
says, 'nd, by Godfrey, them thet's got luck kin hev any
thing else. Thet's what *I've* found."

In short, to put an end to Uncle Shubael's twaddle,
Amaziah went on from bad to worse, lost his schooner
on the rocks off Manhegan; had to go mate of another
man's coaster all winter—no joke, I assure you, to go up

and down our ice-bound coast from Thanksgiving to May-
day, do all the work and have none of the credit—finally,
fell to be cook of a mackerel-catcher, and eked out his
wretched subsistence by digging clams on the beach all
winter, at six dollars a barrel, frozen fingers thrown in.
He worked hard enough, but got to be dreadfully slow—
or, to put it in the Cape vernacular, "it took him a long
time to go an hour." He had a knack of being too late
for every thing, and another knack of always blaming
Providence or some of his acquaintance for this fatality.
Finally, after losing all his friends, and every thing else
he could lose, he died and was buried, fully convinced to
the last moment of his existence that all his misfortunes
were owing to Prudence Robbins refusing him; from the
time of which rejection he dated his uselessness. Peace
to his bones! For such as him there is no resurrection—
I mean, of course, in this life. It must have been a great
relief to him to leave this world, and it certainly was to
his Elmira, who, though she probably liked him from
mere force of habit, had long ceased to hanker after him.

Did it ever occur to you to inquire what was the making of one of your smart men? I don't mean a genius,
but a Yankee; a man for any occasion, who is never too
late, and makes even a losing speculation pay him something? Nine times in ten such a man has had an energetic scold of a mother, and a do-less father. So it was
with Tom—to whom I am right glad to return after this
dreary story of his father.

When Amaziah had the good fortune to die—the only
streak of real luck in his miserable failure of a life—he

left Mrs. Elmira with five children to take care of. It was better than if she had died and left the five to him; but yet it was a hard case. She was not sorry to have the little Tom at least support himself, and this he began to do immediately, by becoming cook of a coaster trading between Boston and New York. Here he was provided for, and could take his monthly six dollars to his mother, who gave him instead good counsel, and, when he needed them, new clothes, ingeniously contrived out of his father's old ones.

Tom had what the Cape men call "'nuity," which means what the rest of America calls "go-a-headativeness"—a barbarous word which no people would coin who did not find it easier to coin money than words. Little as he was, he had felt the multifarious stings of poverty, and now saw the world open before him: his oyster, whose meat he meant surely to taste. And so well did he use his opportunities that at twenty-three he was mate of a China-trader, and at twenty-eight captain and part-owner of one of the finest Indiamen out of Boston.

I have not time to recount here the various fortunes of these intermediate days, but know that his native shrewdness never failed him from the day when, a little shaver of twelve years, he begged a cabin-boy's berth with Captain Nickerson, and by some occult trickery of bargaining which I think he could not himself have explained, got a dollar more per month wages than that close-fisted gentleman had intended to give him, to the day when first he was hailed as Captain Tom.

You are not to think that he achieved his good fortune

without labor. He was not only honest and faithful; he was ever at his post, and always contriving to understand some trick of steering, or stowing, or navigation, which was considerably beyond his years, and to be in the very place where a better man was urgently needed—whereupon Tom incontinently proved himself that better man. Competent servants are always rare, as your wife will tell you, if you have not discovered it for yourself; and it did not a little for Tom that in his various voyages his masters could always put their hands on him when they wanted any body. Moreover, Tom had that kind of spirit which regards the thing just now in hand the best thing in the world. When in his boyhood he swept the ship's decks, he swept as though sweeping were the very noblest work to which the human body and soul could be put; and swept so clean that he wrung reluctant praises from the oldest growler of the forecastle. In fact, Tom was a new broom all the while—and a new broom which does not get old is almost as good as a goose that lays golden eggs. Only, it occurs to me, a man might be something more and better than even a new broom.

Then as he grew up his watch below was devoted to books. Novels sometimes, perhaps, though novels he did not grow to love; they told him nothing. Bowditch rather, and the Nautical Almanac, and M'Culloch's ponderous Dictionary of Commerce, which last was to him the most interesting of books. For he never forgot that some day he was to be captain—and in those four hours of rest he got his education. He knew all about the odd corners of the world; knew how, where, and in what quantities the great commercial staples are produced and used; and one day—it was before he was eighteen—surprised Captain Kelley Howes, busy planning out a new voyage, by the confident announcement that if he would take a cargo of codfish to the Cayenne he would make money.

"Pooh! pooh!" said the Captain. "Go about your business, my boy. Don't be impertinent."

"Hold on," cried the owner, who was present, conferring with the Captain. "What do you mean by such impertinence, Sir—offering advice to your master? Explain. Why do you want fish sent down to French Guiana?"

"They'm Catholics down there, Sir, and they have slaves besides; all Catholics eat fish on Friday, and salt fish is cheaper than meat, in any hot country, for slave-food," answered Tom, sententiously, his face burning at the reproof and his own audacity.

"That'll do! Now clear out, Master Philosopher," said Mr. Sleeper, pushing him off the quarter-deck. But he turned to his Captain, and said, gravely, "You must take care of that lad; some day I'll give him a ship."

He heard nothing further of his impertinent suggestion, but the brig *Cerito* went down to the Spanish main with a load of dried cod, and on her next voyage Tom was her second mate.

They don't doubt of themselves, these Cape boys. I dare say when Tom was twelve he felt himself equal to the command of a seventy-four-gun ship; and what is more, trusting to luck and his native shrewdness, would have carried her safely round the world. They tell a story of him, how when first he was second mate he got himself, by some foolish bragging, a reputation for speaking Spanish. Now the brig was bound to Palermo, and losing a spar on the outward passage, put into Port Mahon to get it replaced. Away goes the Captain to order his yard, but finds the ship-builder ignorant of the English language.

"Send the second mate this way," cried the skipper; "he'll talk to him."

Whereupon enter Tom, with inward trepidation, but much outward brass.

"Tell him I want a new main-yard, and must have it by to-morrow evening."

TOM (*to the Spaniard, with a familiar air*). "Señor, roundy come roundy, and squary come squary : you make a main-yard for John Ingletary ? "

SPANIARD (*amazed*). "No intendez" (I don't understand). And no wonder either.

TOM (*to skipper, with virtuous indignation*). "He says, not in ten days, Sir."

SKIPPER (*enraged*). "Tell him to go to Halifax. We'll hunt up some other man."

And Tom's luck did not fail him; for the next spar-maker they addressed understood English. Now the point and moral of this incident lies here : Tom, having once successfully cheated, did not trust the devil again, but sat himself down to the study of Spanish, and, by the help of an Andalusian whom they shipped at Mahon, could both read and speak it by the next time he passed Gibraltar. A duller fellow would have chuckled over his escape, tried it again, and failed miserably.'

II.

When Prudence Robbins gave to Uncle Amaziah that fatal blow which sent him staggering into the arms of Elmira Rogers, and, as he believed, crippled him for the remainder of his life, one of her motives was this: she loved somebody else. Said somebody was named Isaiah Crowell; and the marriage of Isaiah and Prudence, which took place in due course of courtship, resulted in: little money, considerable happiness, and one daughter, named Mchetabel.

Now one of the earliest playmates of little Hetty was Tom Baker—at that time little bigger. I suppose it was out of some latent kindness for the man who had once offered her all the best of men can offer a woman that Mrs. Prudence showed an especial regard for little Tom, whose happiest hours were spent beneath her roof—who, as Uncle Amaziah sometimes remarked, should have been his mother. The little Mehetabel was a pretty child, and Tom's earliest love affair had her for its object. In fact, until he went to sea, he used to call her his little wife, and when he returned from his voyages he always brought something—a bright handkerchief, a box of figs, a string of coral, some gay sailor gift, redolent of foreign shores—for her; who, meantime, grew persistently prettier, till, at the age of eighteen, she had a face which would have been rarely out of Tom Baker's memory had not business and the thoughts of his career occupied the foremost and most important place there. But I am sure

Mehetabel got more of his thoughts than any thing else but business. ·He no longer dared call her his little wife, and, indeed, got his ears boxed, when, coming home one day, he demanded his usual kiss.

"*She'd* show him that he could not take such liberties with young ladies on the Cape, whatever Mister Impudence might do to the tawny young women he met on his voyages;" wherein she wronged poor Tom sadly, for a more faithful lover (of business and Mehetabel) could not have been, and his career and her fair image kept him unusually free from all temptation of foreign kisses.

Poor Tom! with his sailor innocence of woman's wiles, he was considerably taken aback. Confident of his own love, he had—business-like—taken hers for granted, and had predetermined not to ask formally for her till he got his ship. And now—now, when he felt like immediately having his fate decided for him, he did not dare.

Result: what is commonly known as a lovers' quarrel. Tom sulky: Mehetabel pouting. Tom savage: "Het" ingeniously cruel. Tom determined to go home from singing-school with Het's aversion, Mercy Nickerson: "Het" triumphantly ahead, laughing and talking to Enoch Rogers, Tom's second cousin—a first-class stupid, whom he had already once thrashed for attentions to Mehetabel. Whereupon Tom, humbled, bit the dust, and tried to mollify the saucy beauty by a present of his best Canton silk handkerchief, which was received with a toss of the beautiful head, and a look of the wicked gray eyes, which said, plainly, "*I'll* show you, Mister Impudence."

This time Tom was chief mate. They were bound on a long voyage, and the poor fellow finally determined to tell his love and know his fate before he sailed. What long hours he spent in devising the scene in which the important revelation was to be made! How he determined each day, as his sailing-day drew near, that now, this evening, before he slept, all should be over! How, neglecting the while even the sacred thoughts of business, he rehearsed to himself, shaving before his little round pocket-glass, or walking alone among the scrub pines on the sand-beach, or sailing his boat across the bay, the very words in which he would ask for the great prize! And then, when all was arranged — when the very manner in which the subject of subjects should be introduced was ingeniously devised, and the fatal trap was ready to be sprung—behold! the victim was away! She had a headache, or she had promised to go out with Enoch, or she preferred to stay at home with father and mother: but plainly she had some instinctive perception of what was coming, and avoided it, as women know how to avoid what they do not wish to meet. Day after day Tom lingered in torture, till at last he *must* be off; and, going over to say farewell to Mrs. Prudence and her daughter, now firmly determined to bring matters to some distinct issue, he found Miss Mehetabel—gone to Hyannis to spend a week!

"She'll be sorry not to have bid you good-bye, Tom," said kind Mrs. Crowell; and with this morsel of cold comfort he was obliged to take off his wounded heart Canton-ward.

To tell the truth Mehetabel did not love any one—but especially not him—and she had just begun to discover that fact. She had indeed "liked him well enough"—oh, fatal phrase to lovers!—in that girlhood which was just now ripening into dangerous womanhood. That is to say, he was her earliest playmate, and she was always glad to see him. But in these last years Tom's sober business face, on which the untimely cares and eager ambition of his life had written their hard lines too early, had lost its charm for her. I have noticed that your thoroughly lucky man, who rushes on through the world, conquering and to conquer, mastering every opposing circumstance, winning every point on which he sets his mind, scarce ever gains the woman's heart he loves. For women have an instinctive horror of worldliness—an instinctive jealousy which closes their hearts against the man who may in after-life care less for wife and babies than for bank stock, and live more in Wall Street than in the bosom of his family. "Thou shalt have no other love but mine," says every true woman's heart; and so when your conquering hero confidently assails this last frail fortress of a woman's heart, he finds it impregnable—to him.

So it was with Tom; and while he was going on from luck to luck, and saw himself now presently to be not only rich but honored—while he was eagerly grasping all he could of that good which was to him supreme, behold, Mehetabel was lost to him forever.

There came home one day from sea one Farley Burgess, of whom strange stories were told on the Cape. He

B

had been mate of a ship bound to Rio, and on the outward passage his vessel had foundered and sunk. For
many days they floated about, in a small boat, at the
mercy of the winds and waves; slowly perishing of hunger and thirst; at last lifting ravenous eyes to each other, with dreadful thoughts of what should come to-morrow. Till one glad morning the wretched crew were
picked up by a passing ship. Now, in all these days of
heaviest trial, young Burgess had been the life of his
companions, keeping up their fainting hopes, denying
himself a part of even his small share of bread and water
to comfort his dying captain; in all things a brave, self-
sacrificing, hopeful soul. His shipmates did not speak of
him but with tears in their honest eyes. And now he
was come home, penniless, almost shirtless, to gain some
strength to tempt the deep once more.

I suppose you think they made a hero of him—those
staid old Cape folk? Not they. Heroism is too common with them for that.

"Well, Burgess," said Captain Young, "I hearn ye
had bad luck, boy?"

"Yes, Sir; not so bad's it might ha' been, though."

"Well, well, better luck next time. Heard you held
yourself like a man, though. That's right. Want to
come mackereling with me?"

That was Farley Burgess's welcome home. From the
Cape men, at least; who appreciate manliness readily
enough, but having it also in their own bones, don't fling
up their hats and make speeches when one of their fellows has done his duty man fashion. But the Cape

women—God bless them!—in their quiet hearts Farley Burgess found such welcome that he had never in his life seen so many bright eyes as now rested upon his patched shirt and starved face.

And brightest of all were the gray eyes of Mehetabel Crowell.

Tom's luck was nothing against this man's misfortunes. Tom's smart looks and Canton handkerchiefs stood no chance against Farley's torn clothes and sea-washed face.

And so Tom Baker's fate was decided in his absence.

III.

When he came home Farley and Mehetabel were betrothed. When they should be married was a question of time and luck; for on the Cape young folks must have a house and garden spot of their own before their marriage is like to have the applause of a prudent and comfort-loving public, which has the fear of poverty ever before its eyes.

Tom came home with an easy, self-satisfied swagger, excusable enough in one who at twenty-eight, and without help of rich friends, has achieved the command of an Indiaman. This time a crape shawl was brought for Miss Mehetabel's acceptance; and when offered, was kindly declined.

"Why? It was not seemly for a young girl to accept such presents even from a good friend, as Tom was, and, she hoped, always would be," was Het's timid explanation.

Whereupon Tom refused longer to be called friend, and bluntly demanded right to a dearer title.

And then it all came out. How Mehetabel had always liked Tom, and always would. How she loved some one else. How she had never loved *him.* " Had she ever told him she did ? " she asked, wickedly unable to restrain this little stinging reproof to one who had, it seemed to her, been all too confident of a love which he had taken little care to gain, except by gifts; and Het's cheeks glowed, and her heart grew scornful, as the thought came that perhaps this proud young sultan thought a Canton handkerchief guerdon enough of love.

"And who is the happy man, Miss Mehetabel ? " asked Tom, with a quite perceptible sneer, when he found speech of his rage and surprise.

" Tom," cried Het, bursting into tears, " don't speak so to me! What have I done that you must look so? Did *I* know? Did you ever ask me to love you? *I* never knew you loved any one better than your ship and your voyage. And if I do love Farley Burgess, and he loves me, there's no reason you should be mad ! "

"Farley Burgess, eh? " said Tom, stung beyond self-possession ; " well, I wish you joy of Mr. Farley Burgess, that's all. Good-bye! "   .

And he left poor Mehetabel sobbing, and went home to his little room, locked himself in, and there silently surveyed his defeat.

It strikes men differently, this accident which had just now befallen Captain Tom. For an accident I must call it, seeing that women are the most inconsistent and uncer-

tain of created beings. I have known a man thoroughly humbled by a rejection. Have seen him after, a little
sadder, a little lonelier perhaps, but also a great deal tenderer, wiser, manlier; acquiescing in his fate; acknowl-
edging that he was not worthy this divine blessing of a
true woman's love; but cherishing her memory ever after with a love purer, kinder, nobler, because less selfish
than before: such a love as many a Benedick rises to
only after years of trial and suffering have cleansed him
and made him pure. Giving thereafter to all the world,
but especially to all pure women and little children, this
wealth of love which *she* could afford to do without, and
growing into genial old bachelorhood with the fine grace
of a loving heart ever surrounding and brightening his
life.

Captain Tom was another manner of man. The bit-
terness of death was in his heart as he paced the narrow
floor of his little room. He gnashed his teeth, and swore
great oaths of vengeance for this his first defeat in life.
There is no finer fellow in the world than your prosperous go-ahead man — while fortune favors him, that is.
He acquits himself of life with a graceful swing which
captivates all beholders, of the male sex particularly;
finds it easy enough to be witty or generous; and standing at the top, flings down with gracious complaisance
his penny or his good word to the poor devils below.
Every man gives him his hand, and by very virtue of
his success he gains the air which wins him greater luck.
But beware of this man's first defeat. Napoleon carries
all before him till Waterloo, and then never was so

mean and undignified a prisoner as he. Tom gnashed his teeth in impotent rage. How could he be revenged? and how could he live without his satisfaction? To thrash Farley Burgess was of course the first thought. But then—setting aside the chance that he might not succeed in this so very well—it occurred that this would only make him a laughing-stock to his friends. To marry some one else? Tom smiled sardonically, and vowed eternal hatred, not to this one woman alone, but to all the tribe! What should he do? What could he do? that was the worst.

Pondering which things, he opened a letter from his owners, which that afternoon's mail had brought from Boston. And as he read his face lit up with a smile so devilish in its malignity that now indeed it was evident he had found his revenge.

And so he had. The letter related that his ship was nearly ready. That he would please report himself in Boston in one week from date. That if he could pick up at home three or four good boys it would be well to ship them. That probably Mr. Farley Burgess, whom the owners had engaged as second mate, would be able to give him some assistance in this. That said Burgess had been some time waiting for a berth, and as they knew him to be a trustworthy and intelligent man, they trusted Captain Baker would be pleased with his second officer. That they remained his obedient servants.

"D— him," muttered Captain Tom, crushing the letter in his hand, " I've got him now."

Tom had him sure enough. He was abundantly satisfied—so he wrote the owners—and as for Farley, even if he had not been satisfied, which, knowing nothing of the storm he had raised in his Captain's heart, was not the case, Tom knew he would not back out.

I need not stop to recount all the guileless ways in which poor Mehetabel sought to mollify the rage of her lost lover—to show him what he would by no means see, that he alone was in fault; to win from him one good word, or insinuate into his hard heart one kindly thought of her he had so professed to love. Tom cherished his hatred, his sense of injury received and revenge due, as men always cherish the devil when he has secured a snug corner in their hearts. " His old luck had not failed him yet," he said to himself, " for what could be luckier than to have his arch-enemy at this vantage ? "

Poor Mehetabel had little comfort of her love. For she knew, better than you do, probably, fair reader, how thoroughly indeed Tom had Burgess in his power. At best the second mate of a ship is only the chief drudge. The first on deck and the last to leave it; the first to put his hand to every mean toil; the first to leap to every place of peril; the first to be blamed if any thing goes wrong; the last to receive credit if all goes right.

It is no small matter to hold creditably this post, which demands, for the wages of a porter, all the manual skill of the finest old sailor; all the energy and endurance of a dray horse ; all the judgment, knowledge, and fertility of resource necessary to command a man-of-war. Then consider that the autocrat who holds in his hands the few morsels of comfort left to this luckless mortal is his deadly enemy, and has not only power and will, but time, place, and opportunity, to wreak upon him every small indignity, every discomforting annoyance which the devil of ingenuity can prompt. No wonder poor Mehetabel carried her anxious face over to old Mrs. Baker's, and humbled herself in vain efforts to make it up with Tom.

IV.

And so the good ship *Melchior* sailed.

Do you know what they call " hazing " at sea? Hazing is the art of tormenting systematized; it is making a man unhappy without breaking his bones; it is adroitly robbing him of every privilege and comfort which the law does not in so many words secure him; heaping upon him every indignity short of that last point where even prudent men come to blows; artfully indulging every other man that this man's complaints may find no backers: in short, it is making of the narrow decks of an Indiaman such a hell that many a good man has been hazed overboard to cool his agony in a watery grave; and many another, less lucky, has been hazed into murdering his hazer—whereupon the majesty of the law steps in and virtuously strings him up. This is hazing. They say our American captains are good at it. I have known one or two who were. There was Captain Carver—but he was a fool.

And to this work Captain Tom—dead and damned if ever a living man was in this world—now devoted long days and studious nights. The sore which festered at his heart left him no peace, no rest, no joy. His black face, not scowling, but carrying ever a fine devilish sneer, cast its gloom even to the bows of the old ship, whose good heart of oak had surely never before carried such an infernal load as this.

And truly he hazed Farley Burgess.

The Highland light was not yet out of sight when the work began. The foretop-sail was to be reefed, and Captain Tom, well knowing that if at this first reefing match the second mate did not get his weather earing he would be disgraced forever with the crew, by various subterfuges kept him aft till the gear was hauled out and the men were in the rigging. This time, though, Farley was too much for him, for, springing on the yard, he ran out over the men's heads, to their no slight admiration, and took his place of honor.

But this was only a beginning, and Captain Tom was not the man to be defeated on his own deck. Day and night he found fault. If the log was not written up at the exact time; if the ship was steered badly; if too much or too little sail was made; if the wind changed suddenly, and she was not at once put about, down he came on the second mate. He refused new rope, and when a halyard carried away called Mr. Burgess to account. He deprived the morning watch of their six o'clock coffee, and contrived that the second mate should bear the blame. The starboard watch always holy-stoned the decks—by his secret orders to Burgess—while the mate's watch simply washed down ; and thus

B 2

poor Burgess fell into bad odor with his crew, as one
who tried to "curry favor" with the Captain. *He* curry
favor! He lingered over his dinner, in pleasant converse
with the mate, knowing that meantime the second mate's
dinner was spoiling. Shall I tell you more of the small,
maddening tyrannies of the sea? No; let it suffice that
the devil need want no better position to wreak his spite
on any poor human soul than this of Captain Tom's:
autocrat of an Indiaman; lord of all he surveys; holding
a power of more than life and death over the wretches
who *must* go when he says go, come when he says come,
and stand silent when his lordship, moved by indiges-
tion, or a broken night's slumber, vents his spleen upon
them.

Let it suffice, that, whatever artifice any malignant
genius could suggest, Captain Tom unscrupulously used
to bring his second mate into contempt, and to make his
life thoroughly wretched. Always stopping short, remember, at that point—very far off, indeed, on shipboard
—where resistance becomes a virtue: though not even
then a lawful virtue. For bear in mind that, under our
blessed laws, your Captain may starve you, may curse
you, may beat you, may force you to peril your life beyond hope of salvation, and you may not resist—may
not even remonstrate. You may sue for damages—that
is, if you survive, and your tyrant does not leave the
ship at Sandy Hook, and disappear till you have gone
to sea again to keep bread in your mouth, as some of our
"Bully" New York captains used to do, and do now,
for aught I know.

And Farley Burgess bore it all. Patiently, silently: only not defiantly, for he felt that if it once came to defiance, actual battle would be imminent — and then — Mehetabel. How he repined over the hard fate which tied his hands, and bound him, an honorable brave man, every inch a sailor, to bear, unresisting, the contumely of such a master! Once, indeed, he ventured on a word. They lay in Canton River, opposite Whampoa; and Farley said—

"Captain Baker, you don't seem to be satisfied with me."

"Yes, Sir," replied Tom, with a gleam of malignant triumph in his eyes, "I am satisfied; why?"

"You don't show it, Sir; and I have to say that if you want to be rid of me, you need only make out my discharge."

"No, Sir; if you don't like your berth you may desert. I don't think I shall look for you. But I'm satisfied." And the cool villain turned away.

Of course Burgess could not desert, and thus stain his fair fame at home with bride and owners.

The passage home was just as bad. There was no relenting in Captain Tom, who, to tell the truth, was getting such a habit of abusing his second mate that he would have found it difficult to leave off. Day by day his heart grew blacker with the hate he so carefully nourished. Day by day as he himself grew more wretched, he found more pleasure in hazing Burgess. But even a passage home must come to an end. I scarce know what was in these men's hearts, toward each other, as they approached once more their native shores. Captain Tom thought only of the present, and probably gave no heed to the day of reckoning which was approaching. And Burgess? "I'll thrash this beast, in Boston, till every bone of his body cries for mercy." This was what honest Farley Burgess said to himself fifty times a day, counting eagerly every mile the good ship bore him on his way to liberty and revenge. For even an honorable brave man may be imbruted by such persistent devilishness as Captain Tom's.

And now they near the land. Still no let-up from Captain Tom. And now they see the land, the old Highland of Cape Cod; and to-morrow Farley Burgess means, "God willing," to give this his tyrant such a warning as will go far to make a man of him, if he survives.

"God willing."

They had been slowly drifting all night, and just caught a glimpse of the land in the dim distance, as the morning sun rose fiery out of the ocean and plunged into the other sea, of clouds, which waited his appearance to hang out their colors of fierce portentous scarlet and crimson.

> " Sunrise red in the morning,
>   Sailors take warning."

chanted old Harry Hill, a sturdy croaker of the forecastle, who, by dint of persistently foretelling ill-luck, now and then got himself the reputation of a prophet.

"Never heed the warning," replied Burgess. " To-morrow night you'll sleep softer than you've done this year past, old Harry, in your snug Sailors' Home."

All day they drifted down upon the land—no wind, but only a rapid tide setting the ship with no small speed along the bending shore, till at last it seemed they must round the Race, and drift past Wood End, fairly into Provincetown harbor.

Better they had.

Toward night a slight breeze was felt from the southward, and spreading all studding-sails, threatening as it looked, Captain Tom urged the good ship on.

But scarcely were the studding-sails set when the breeze chopped round to the north. The great white clouds which had rolled over and over along the horizon all day, rose, as by magic, and covered the whole sky; the wind came in sharp puffs, each stronger than the last; and by the time the topsails were close-reefed there blew a gale from the north, beneath which the old ship lay down almost to her beam ends.

When they had once more time to look round, they found themselves where they should not have been caught in this gale. The land of the Cape trends by a long slow curve from the Highland light to the west and south; and by a shorter semicircle, from the Race, forms the landlocked harbor of Provincetown. Between the Race and the Highland is a stretch of high bluff, with a narrow beach running along its foot, and this, from its shape, is known to navigators as the "back." of the Cape—the place where many a good homeward-bound ship has laid her bones to bleach. Now, while the *Mel-*

chior lay becalmed, the tide, which runs along here like a mill-race, had set her imperceptibly past the Race, and left her with this fatal " back " dead under her lee.

There was no time for deliberation. Putting the ship on the port tack, Captain Tom shook a reef out of his main and foretop-sails, set his whole foresail and reefed mainsail, and sending the best man to the helm, sought to drive her past the bluff point which now loomed fearfully near, through the dark gloom of the night.

" If only the tide favored us," sighed he to himself. But the deadly tide of the Race favors no man.

On she forged, groaning grievously under the tremendous pressure of her canvas, which sent her headlong into vast seas, each one of which it seemed must be her tomb. The men held on about the quarter-deck—there was no living, forward—and with set faces awaited the event, powerless to do more. The officers stood aft, watching the helmsman; scanning close the sails and rigging, fearful lest some overstrained piece of cordage might give way and plunge all into ruin. Captain Tom, silent, grim, every nerve braced, every sense alive to the occasion, held by the mizzen rigging, now watching the red glare of the light, which shone almost down upon his decks, now commanding the helmsman to " ease her when she pitches— you'll have the masts out of her next! "—as though old Harry Hill had not steered a frigate ère now, in as tight a place as this.

" We don't gain much, Sir," shouted Mr. Falconer, the chief mate, in the Captain's ear, pointing to the high bluff which already seemed overtopping the masts, and from whose edge the fearful glare of the light-house light seemed calmly eying them, as some one-eyed Polyphemus waiting for the prey which should be surely his.

"No, Sir, we lose," was Captain Tom's reply; "set the mizzen topsail, close-reefed, and go out, some one, and loose the jib!"'

The men looked aghast. Five or six sprang to prepare the mizzen topsail; but no one moved forward.

"Loose the jib! d'ye hear there? What are ye waiting for?" shouted Tom, chafing at the delay.

"No man can lie out on that boom and live, Sir," said an old seaman, touching his forelock; and as he spoke a solid green sea boarded her over the bows, submerging bowsprit and jib-boom, and swept aft an avalanche of water, bearing before it caboose, water-casks, every thing movable on deck—ready witness to the impossibility.

"Loose the jib, I tell ye!" shouted Captain Tom. "Who says *can't* here? Let me hear it once!"

But as he spoke a form was seen struggling out on the bowsprit, and, bewildered and cowed, the crew lay forward to hoist away. In the din of waters no voice could be heard, and no soul knew who was the daring fellow who had risked all at their mad Captain's word, till, as her bows were lifted on a vast wave, Farley Burgess made one mighty leap from the bowsprit end, and landed fairly on the top-gallant forecastle. So the jib was set.

And still the fiery eye looks down upon them through the storm, calm, inscrutable as fate, in the midst of the raging gale, only waiting, waiting for the hapless prey

which vainly struggles in the toils. And now the hollow
boom of the surf becomes dimly audible amid the groaning and creaking of the timbers, the wild shrieking of the
gale, and the fierce rush of the mighty sea.

"I hear it!" shrieked Captain Tom to his mate, "I hear
it! But if all holds we'll drive her by yet!" And standing on his own deck there, he looked, in this last extremity, happier, better, than he had looked or felt these many
months.

If all holds! But what is that? With a sound as of
a sudden thunder-crash, the brand-new main-topsail splits,
and in a moment is blown into a hundred thousand shreds.

"My God!"

"Mind your helm! Ease her! Ease her now!"

Too late! No human hand can ease her now. The
surf has her; and as she feels the fierce, passionate jerk
of the under-tow, as she is pitched, and tossed, and twisted
in the relentless grasp, a mere chip in this maelstrom, a
straw in the torrent of Niagara, Captain Tom's voice
is heard, ringing out above even this thunderous roar,
"Hold fast, every body!"

And none too soon. For, rising for the last time in
her life on a vast, towering, foam-topped billow, the good
old ship is hurled crashing to her doom. Down, down,
down! Will she never stop? It is but half a second:
it seems many minutes to those who, with clenched teeth
and streaming hair, cling to the shrouds, till, with a shock
as of two planets meeting, she strikes the beach!

"God help my poor men!" sobbed Captain Tom, as he
felt himself torn from his firm grasp of the rigging, and

slung far into the seething caldron of waters; slung out into the surf, where, for a moment striking out, there comes a great blinding shock, as though his head were splitting, and then Captain Tom closes his eyes, folds his hands, and knows no more.

Meantime, a more fortunate wave had cast six half-drowned men upon the narrow beach; to whom, just collecting their scattered senses, crawled slowly the second mate.

"How many are we here? Thank God!" exclaimed he. Then scarce waiting to get a little breath, he gathered himself to the rescue of his drowning shipmates.

"Here, hold this line." With wise forethought Burgess had tied about his body a small strong line of considerable length, and with this about him, gathering a few hasty breaths of spray-laden air, he now rushed back into the roaring surf, intent on saving whom he might; but first of all his enemy—his Captain.

Once he returns, bearing the lifeless body of the steward.

A second time, and the boiling surge gives up to him a half-drowned seaman.

Again, and yet no Captain.

Yet once more! Breaking from the men, he rushes in to grasp what may come to his hands. Buffeted, blinded, only half conscious himself, they are already pulling him back, when his fingers close mechanically on the hair of one dashed by on the long sweep of an outward-bound wave. With the grasp of death he holds his prize, and drags out Captain Tom.

Lifeless? Yes. No; but faintly breathing, and sore-ly wounded. Carry him up! And Burgess, forgetting his own exhaustion, no longer remembering his bitter enmity, bears the limp body to a sheltered spot, strips his few rags to protect it from the cold blast, binds up its wounds, and cares for its flickering life.

When Captain Tom opened his eyes it was day. He was lying on the wreck-strewn beach, a half-dozen sea-drenched sleepers near him, sole survivors of his brave crew; the second mate keeping silent watch.

"Is this all, Mr. Burgess?" he mustered strength to ask.

"All, Sir."

"I'm hurt, I find. But you might have saved more, Sir. I hope you did your duty," said Captain Tom.

The old devil had not been washed out of him yet.

Burgess made no reply, for his Captain sank back, exhausted, and slept.

V.

On the 15th of last June the little village church of Dennis was crowded, chiefly with women and children, the men being mostly off fishing, to witness the marriage of Captain Farley Burgess with Miss Mehetabel Crowell. The ceremony had been performed, the short prayer was ended, and friends were advancing to congratulate the newly married, when a wagon drove up to the door, and Captain Tom Baker, grim, pale, and with a huge scar across his forehead, a memento of his shipwreck, advanced slowly and painfully up the aisle. Now Captain Tom had not been seen at home since the wreck; and knowing his former feelings toward Mehetabel, his presence here was embarrassing to all, who easily conjectured that he could come hither unbidden on no pleasant errand.

And truly it was no pleasant errand to him. Looking neither to right nor left, he walked to the altar, and there, lifting his hat, said:

"Good friends, when a man has publicly done wrong, been mean and cowardly and devilish, it is right that he should publicly confess his sins and ask forgiveness; and I for one find he'll get no peace otherwise. Here's my shipmate, Farley Burgess, to whom I have done every mean spite that I could work out, and who repaid all by saving my life—whom I abused after he had saved me and cared for me—and who never gave me a word of reproach. I've come to ask you, Burgess, to forgive me if you can, and to make me feel like an honest man once more, by giving me your hand in token that you forgive and forget. God knows, I see the meanness of my life, and—"

More he would have said, the stern proud man, but Farley stepped forward, and grasping him by the hand, led him to where Mehetabel stood, a blushing bride, then said: "God bless you, Tom Baker; I knew there was a man's heart in you!"

And Mehetabel, lifting up her sweet tearful eyes, said only, "Brother Tom?"

But Brother Tom had lost his voice, and had such a

choking feeling in his throat, that, pale and weak as he was, Hetty had to support him on her arm; and, Burgess holding his other arm, they walked down the broad aisle to the little porch of the church.

And there stood Uncle Shubael—just arrived, who, beholding this trio, exclaimed:

"God bless my soul! Captain Tom Baker? When did *you* come to life?"

"Just now, in the church," was Tom's reply, turning to Farley and his bride.

WHAT IS BEST?

WHAT IS BEST?

I.—WHICH IS PRELIMINARY.

I HOPE every body who sets out to read this story is familiar with the little child's game called "Simon." There is a kind of philosophy in all games, as there is in every thing else, if we could but see it; and this in particular has struck me as a comical parody on that more mature game of "Follow my leader," which all the world delights to play at, whether the leader be Napoleon, or Mr. Genio C. Scott who does the fashion-plates with so admirable a grace.

But I do not mean to drag the game of Simon in here on account of any philosophical principles which a crotchety man might pick out of it, as Jerseymen pick pearls from decayed clams. The less as, like some stupid Jerseymen, I should most likely cook my clam, and thus spoil my pearl. "Simon" comes appositely to me, because the man of whom I am about to write sometimes seemed to me the veritable "old original" Simon —the ideal Simon, of whom all other five-year-old Simons are but the faint reflex; and because in this person's career I seem to detect certain progressive phases which are like nothing so much as the consecutive development of a well-played game of "Simon."

It is as well to say here, at the beginning, that the hero of this story is what we call in America a "literary man."

I have noticed that the American public is very fond of gossip about the private lives of great writers. When the beloved Irving died, there was scarce one of us poor devils but remembered or invented some pleasant little anecdote illustrative of his genial character; and even his family physician entered the lists with a pathetic and pathologic description of the disease to which the dear old gentleman succumbed; as though Providence had provided a special and entirely novel extinguisher to put out the lamp of so great a genius, leaving the vulgar rush-lights of us common scribblers to be snuffed out in the usual way—with the fingers, so to speak. Now, it is of no use to kick against the pricks; and as it is so evidently the highest duty and business of a writer to please his public, I have determined to communicate here some passages, hitherto unnoted, in the life of the only distinguished writer whose history it has been my good fortune to know.

I met him first one evening at a party given by my good friend, Mr. Brown, in the Fifth Avenue (New York). I was listening to some of the brilliant sallies of the celebrated editor, and part proprietor, of the New York *Daily Golden Egg*, when he suddenly ceased speaking, and looking over my right shoulder towards a middle-aged, compactly - built, comfortable - looking man, said—

"Do you know who that is?"

"That?" said I; "no."

"That," said he, "is one of the great editorial lights of this country, and a most successful writer. It is the celebrated MacGurdigan."

"Is it possible!" I exclaimed. "Do I see before me" —I had turned about, and was now facing the renowned personage—"do I see before me the great Stoffle Mac-Gurdigan?"

Then, seized with an irresistible desire to know intimately one of the most remarkable men our country has produced, I said, catching the hand of my friend the editor—

"My dear Goose, do me a great favor: introduce me to a man whom I have so long and so greatly admired."

Goose, who is as amiable socially as he is valorous editorially, at once complied with my wish.

We were introduced to each other! I shook the hand which had penned lines whose matchless eloquence, stern patriotism, and great moral purpose have, in my humble opinion, never been excelled—no, not even by the immortal Tupper. The lustrous eyes of genius beamed a kindly look upon me. Need I add that I was happy?

It is the fate of greatness to be troubled by littleness. It is a misfortune that at our great parties undisturbed intellectual conversation, which is so delightful between friends, is almost impossible. (Mrs. Betsey, my wife, re-

C

marks here, parenthetically, that great parties are not given to promote precisely this object—but that is nei- ther here nor there.) I was listening with rapt attention to the words of my distinguished friend, hoping to catch some sentence which I should treasure up hereafter, and perhaps publish at his death, in a little biographical sketch, when some intrusive and ill-mannered person touched him lightly on the arm, and, ere he could remon- strate, bore him off to a distant part of the room.

Thus concluded my first and only meeting with a man who is so often admired among the foremost of those few who have shed such a lustre upon our country's journalism.

And thus we complete this preliminary division of our history, and come, without further delay, to the story itself—of which, however, I must first be permit- ted to say, that as the revelations I am about to make are necessarily sometimes unpleasant to the person spoken of—as are many revelations which the intelligent public buys and reads with the utmost avidity—and as I should grieve to have the revered MacGurdigan suspect me as the cause of any pain he may suffer in this case, I have requested the respectable editor of *Harper's Maga- zine* to withhold my name from those emissaries of the goddess of Fame who, as I am informed, call upon him monthly to gain the knowledge which enables them to praise or damn impartially each article as it appears, and without the preliminary trouble of reading it. For though, as a rule, I abhor the absurd anonymous system now in vogue in the Magazines—whereby one man becomes as good as another, and sometimes a great deal better—I own that in peculiar cases, as this, it has its con-venience.

And thus we come at last to the beginning of the game,

II.—IN WHICH "SIMON SAYS SHOW YOUR HANDS."

STOFFLE MACGURDIGAN, Esquire, was born in Peoria, a place which has furnished most of our country's great men. This fact is not a very important one; but it is the duty of a biographer, not only to be fully informed, but also to make evident this fullness to his readers; and moreover, the Peorians, among whom this Magazine has a great circulation, will feel flattered by the mention of their cherished home in its pages.

It was while he was at college that young Stoffle gave the first indications of genius. These preliminary sparks· were drawn out by a young lady of the place, whom the boys used to call a flame of his. She was a pretty girl, Lucy Jones by name, who had been predestined by her parents to catch an under-graduate; and who made the best of her fate by wounding and capturing that one who seemed to her the finest fellow in the class which was the senior when Cupid lent her his bow and arrows.

There were twenty-six seniors to choose out of; and she chose Stoffle.

There were sixty-nine marriageable young ladies to choose from (leaving out of the account twenty-five who had already made up their minds, and one hundred and thirty-three who were yet in short dresses, and flirted with the juniors, and made faces at the sophomores). And Stoffle chose Lucy Jones.

Whose love was the greatest?

Young men dream dreams; and all the more and all the better when they have young women to help them. These two, you may be sure, went into the castle-building line very strongly.

They were poor: and surely there is no such architect as poverty.

They were deeply in love: and surely there is no such decorator as love.

They were young: and surely there is no such landscape gardener as youth.

What splendid castles they did build! What superb views! What magnificent distances! For in Spain, you must know, every castle is placed on top of a mountain; and though the view immediately below is somewhat obstructed by a kind of pleasant Indian-summery haze, if you look far enough away every thing at once becomes clear and bright, and as glorious—as glorious as you please to imagine it.

In the midst of this castle-building the senior year was drawing to a close, and the question What to do? began to urge itself with an irritating pertinacity which interfered a good deal with the pleasures of architecture. When a young man has the world before him to choose from, and a pretty girl's happiness depending on his choice, it is not so easy to decide what is best. There were projects—and projects. Of course Stoffle was not going to be a shoe-maker. They do not waste four years in college to fit themselves for shoe-making—I wish they did. And this being thus out of the question, there remained only the ministry, for which Stoffle did not feel a particular "call;" medicine, which involved three or four years further study, and an indefinite postponement of connubial bliss; and the law: but think of the lawyers' shingles, thick as clap-boards in a Down-East village, which disfigure all our business streets! And then—

"Why then, of course! why did not we think of it before? was not Stoffle the best writer in his class? and was not there literature?"

To be sure—that was just it! It *is* such a comfort, just when you have stumbled upon a dreadful dilemma with three horns, each of which looks disagreeably sharp, to come suddenly upon a fourth horn which is two-pronged, and receives you in its soft embrace without trouble or goring.

So there was literature, and Stoffle should be a literary man. That was settled at any rate. Then by and by he would write essays and books, which would give him reputation; and some day he would come back and lecture before the Lyceum in the old college-town, and would not that be fame? and would not that be happiness? thought dear Lucy Jones; who had a very beautiful castle built in a minute, on the very highest peak in all Spain, and standing on its roof looked all over the world at once, and saw only everywhere, covering the sky above and the trees below, large posters announcing in red letters that "Stoffle MacGurdigan, Esquire, the

celebrated author and popular lecturer, would deliver the
opening lecture of the course on" and so forth, and so
forth.

Now there is a vagueness about this term "literary
man," which is exceedingly charming to almost every
body. "What does so-and-so do?" "Oh, he is a literary man!" And then you have settled the matter.
That includes fame, and money, and friends, and influence, and every other kind of happiness that the very
robust imagination of full-blooded youth can think out.

As for bread and butter and new shoes for the baby—
in Spain, it is well known, all the forests are full of bread-
and-butter trees; and as for baby's shoes, why bless
your dear soul, you must not look so very far ahead. Is
it not known that every book makes the fortune of its
author? Did not Cooper build a town? Did not Mrs.
Stowe go to Europe in state? And are there not
"Homes of American authors," dear cozy places, with
old-time traditions, and ivy, and flowers, and a lawn, and
a carriage-house in the distance? And shall there be no
more cottages on the Hudson?

Nevertheless, if you look into the matter a little, you
will find that Professor Longfellow is a teacher; and Mr.
Bryant is an editor; and Mr. Hawthorne was very glad
to exchange the "Old Manse" for Salem Custom-House,
and that for the Liverpool Consulate; while I—if you
must know it, Madame, I am a tailor. A fashionable
tailor, of course; none of your vulgar snips. When you
go down to Franklin Square, the Editor of *Harper's Magazine* will be glad to hand you my business card; and if

you meet him going to church on fine Sundays, you can
see one of my most stylish coats—and please to call your
husband's attention to the graceful swing of the tails. It
is a new cut, invented for me by a poor devil in my establishment, and which I have patented.

So dear Stoffle should be a literary man. That was
certainly best; and when it was settled a great weight of
responsibility was taken off Lucy's mind. For, of course,
she felt responsible for Stoffle's future; and this vexa-
tious question of "What to do?" had given her some
sleepless nights. And now it was settled so nicely!

For, after all, lawyers are notoriously selfish creatures,
and often have to make wrong right, and right wrong;
and physicians seem to grow callous to suffering, and besides never have a real spare hour, and may be called out
at any time of night, which is not comfortable to look
forward to. And as for preaching, to be sure that is to
be great and good: but then preachers *are* a little stiff
and all that; and society forbids them to dance and do
other pleasant things which society does not deny itself.
But a "literary man!" That was just the thing! There
was leisure, and culture, and freedom. And what a noble field for doing good! thought dear sweet Lucy Jones.

Of course the thing was out of the question, because I
was only a beginner in business then, and had but a small
shop in a poor street, and was not yet famous for my cut
or for my occasional literary labors; and Lucy Jones and
her people would have laughed in my face had they suspected it: but in those days, when Lucy's nice face went
past my shop window, with a kind of sweet glory of

humble happiness and sunny glad good-nature lining her
bonnet, I used to wish that I too was a senior in college;
and my heart would go pitapat, and my needle *would* jag
my fingers, in spite of myself.   I was even ass enough
once to trust her brother for a suit of my best broadcloth,
and lost my bill, as I deserved.   Of course I do not bear.
malice toward Lucy.   But that is neither here nor there,
as I tell Mrs. Betsey when she wants to interfere with the
shop—as the best of women will sometimes.

"What a noble field for doing good!" said Lucy to Stoffle, as they talked over his future, which was now so
pleasantly settled.   So many wrongs in the world yet to
put down with his brave and eloquent pen.   So many
brave thoughts, which should strengthen the weak and
encourage the weary on the way of life.   So wide a field!
and then she felt, away down in her loving heart, a secret
fear, by no means to be expressed lest it should discour-
age this puissant young knight—a secret fear lest all the
wrongs should be righted ere he could fairly buckle on
his armor and make ready to charge with his goose-quill,
lest the devil should die before this, her saint, got one
good blow at him.

A few weeks before Commencement they called together one evening at the house of the President, the
Reverend Doctor Wiseacre; and how Lucy's heart beat
when the kind old gentleman, whom every young man
and maiden in the town loved as a father, said, "Well,
Stoffle, pretty soon now you'll leave us.   Have you determined what career to make for yourself, my dear
boy?"

Stoffle hesitated a little, as was natural; but finally brought out his determination to take to literature.

The old gentleman's face shone with pleasure. "That is a noble thought," said he. "I wish more of our young men would turn their attention to letters. Business is very well, and for the majority commerce or a lucrative profession is best. But I sorrow to see the best minds I train up go out to seek gold, as though California were the nearest cut to heaven, and eagles the only birds to carry men to Paradise."

"And what branch of letters or study do you intend to pursue?" asked the old Doctor, presently.

"That is what I would be glad to have your advice on, Sir," said Stoffle, blushing.

There was a little pause, while the Doctor bent his head down and gently rubbed his eyebrows with his out-stretched fingers—his way of exciting ideality and the other intellectual organs which phrenologists assure us lie near those parts.

"Well, my boy," was the reply after this little pause, "you have your living to make while you build up for yourself that edifice of fame from whose summit you will one day look down on us all. I think I should, if I were in your place, seek a connection with the daily press. It is not difficult, I believe, for an educated young man, of good moral character, and who comes well recommended (as it will be my care to see that you are), to obtain the place of reporter on a daily journal."

Stoffle looked down in silence and evident disappoint-ment.

"A reporter!" exclaimed Lucy, who, though listening to Mrs. Wiseacre, had not lost a word of the other conversation. "Oh, Doctor! a reporter! why, Stoffle is going to be a poet!"

"All in good time, my dear," was the reply; "all in good time. We must not begin at the top of the ladder, you know; else the first step would be the last, and we should lose all the pleasure and advantage of the ascent."

"But a reporter!" reiterated Lucy, with a pretty pout; "why, any body can be a reporter!"

"My dear child," said the Doctor, "draw your stool up here. There, sit down just here; I want to tell you something." And looking kindly into the young girl's upturned face, and smoothing her fair hair, as she sat at his feet, the Reverend Doctor Wiseacre said:

"The daily newspaper of our day, my dear, is the Iliad of our age—only written up journal-wise, and by fifty Homers instead of one. Before you say 'only a reporter,' think for a moment what is the work of which this lowly worker is to do his share. Consider the mighty influence of this daily press—which has been called the Fourth Estate in England, where the London *Times*, by its Jove-like omnipotence of sway, has earned itself the name of *Thunderer*. Note how daily it brings all the affairs of all the world before that little world of highest intelligence which shapes the destinies of a century. See how its private enterprise shames the tardiness of government expresses, and corrects the blunders of official mismanagement. Read how daily it makes public what rogues and fools vainly strive to conceal; and giving honest news to all the world, thereby prevents those cheating combinations and wicked monopolies in politics and trade by which selfish men are ever ready to war against society for their own advantage. See this *Times*, or one of our own great dailies, marching on in its course, steadfast and calm, unmoved by the eager pressure of party interests, undismayed by the awful front of sudden and unlooked-for calamities; and in times of trouble, when events seem to have broken loose, and the majority of men are looking on with bewildered minds, incapable of right thought or judicious action, see this great guide and helmsman of the State moving unflinchingly in his course, never heeding the clamors of demagogues or the pulings of cowards; blown about by no stray winds of doctrine; holding ever his grand faith, that a principle is of more value and of greater power than any multitude of interests : possessing his iron soul in patience; willing to wait; believing in God; knowing that men strive vainly against His laws, and that only truth is simple, only truth is useful, only truth can conquer. Let us thank God that this daily paper is indeed not only the guide and helmsman of our civilization, but truly its ruler.; ·the general who leads the front of battle—or, better (for this is but a sorry comparison), the architect who guides, according to the immutable principles of the universe, the innumerable army of workmen who are ever adding stone after stone to the great temple of our modern Christian Democratic Civilization.

" What are kings and councillors to this *Times*, which makes public their secrets before they have themselves guessed them? What are Presidents and would-be Presidents, eagerly seeking to mislead the public will to their own short-sighted and perverse theories—misstating facts and falsifying history—to this faithful monitor, who from his calm eminence speaks daily truth to waiting millions; with his little pellet of fact blows to the winds the fine-spun theories of scheming politicians; with his Drummond-light of common sense clears the horizon, however darkened by clouds of lies? How impotent the power of the mightiest self-seeking against this simple engine, whose daily breath is that never-perishing voice of the people, which is so truly the voice of God! What Neapolitan dungeon of the Inquisition does not open to its talismanic touch? What secret of tyranny is safe from its searching gaze? What perfidious treason can gain head so long as this thousand-eyed watchman sits faithful at his post?

"The people which possesses but one such free press, honest, incorruptible, and sensible, is safe against all the mysteries of tyranny and all the wicked devices of misplaced ambition. One such free press may work a Revolution, one such free press may inspire a Reformation. As indeed, to my mind, old Luther was himself the father of daily journalism—the man who first proved to the world the vast power of an honest word, spoken in season and out of season, repeated to-day, reiterated to-morrow, spread everywhere, educating every man, even the lowest peasant, to think for himself. The constantly recurring numberless pamphlets of Luther were the germ of which our daily paper is the full-grown fruit; and

Brother Martin was himself a model editor, scorning no topic, if only it illustrated a truth; thinking no game too small, nor too large; awed by no threats of consequences, to himself or to the world; puzzled by no sophistries; keeping fast hold of his torch of truth, brandishing it unceasingly in the faces of her opponents, and never swerving a hair's-breadth—in whatever hideous and devilish uproar—from that grand and simple faith in right, and in God, the father and defender of right, which alone upheld him, against Popes and Emperors and Kings, and all the forces which Satan anxiously brought forward to put down the terrible monk!

"Thus does the office of editor seem to me, my dear, the highest and noblest which a man may nowadays aspire to. He is the wise and brave general of an army in which the reporter is, to be sure, but a humble private—but remember that here, as in Napoleon's legions, every private (besides his rations of frugal but sufficient bread and cheese) carries in his knapsack a marshal's staff. 'Only a reporter,' my dear? Think again, if it is not an office worthy and ennobling in itself—even if it were not the first step on the way to the potent editorial chair; which I am sure no one will reach more speedily, or fill more worthily, than our Stoffle."

"Dearie me, what a lecture, Doctor!" exclaimed Mrs. Wiseacre. "I'm sure I thought you were scolding poor dear Lucy. Don't mind him, my dear. I don't believe you understood half he said."

But Lucy did comprehend and believe all she had just heard; and with a soft sigh of regret at the vanishing picture of Stoffle the poet, she turned with new hopes to the just rising image of Stoffle the editor.

"I am content, dear Sir, if only Stoffle thinks it best," said she, in her sweet, humble way, asking nothing for herself, but only for her hero.

And he, now seeing for the first time a practical opening into that jealous oyster, the world, was no less content to be "only a reporter"—determining in his secret heart, however, to give still some spare hours to the Muse.

Thus was brought about Stoffle MacGurdigan's connection with the daily press, but for which I should have lacked a hero for this story; and thus we come to Part

III.—IN WHICH "SIMON SAYS UP."

I am not sure but the good old President made himself a little ridiculous to well-informed readers (if I should chance to have such), when he expressed a belief that educated young men, of good moral character, and coming well recommended, were especially eligible to reporters' places on the Daily Press. The fact is, in the country a New York daily looks like a very tremendous affair, with a very tremendous purpose, and conducted with prodigious and never hesitating wisdom in all its branches; and simple country people, like the Reverend Doctor Wiseacre, reasoning with too much literalness from apparent effects to quite impossible causes, easily persuade themselves that the *Daily Golden Egg* really contains a healthy embryo chick. In which belief they are confirmed by

the persistent cackle of the editor, who, remembering that
the voices of his family once saved Rome, magnanimously
cackles away, for dear life, resolved that if Republics can
be saved by so slight a means as this, ours shall at least
last out his life-time.

To prevent disappointment, and to keep away from the
city the armies of well-educated young men with good
moral characters, who so greatly abound in the rural dis-
tricts, I think it proper to give notice that the Reverend
Doctor Wiseacre was misinformed; and that no opening
of the kind promises itself to the precise characters speci-
fied—who will find their best opportunities in the whaling
service, where their work will be healthier and a trifle
more dangerous, but no dirtier.

A good character is of very little importance in the
city. And this not because we do not regard such things,
dear friends, but because here, in the metropolis, every
body—even the Mayor—is eminently respectable; and
there is such an abundance of this moral gold that it has
long ago ceased to be a medium of exchange, and is scarce
thought now to have even a commercial value. I may
add that brass, which much resembles it, passes current
far more readily; but this is a hint which will perhaps
be needless to the country reader.

Thus when Stoffle came to New York to try his fortune, it was not his sheep-skin certificate of scholarship,
nor his very numerous vouchers of good moral character
which gained him his first opportunity, but the discovery
that he was an adept in the crooked mysteries of short-
hand, and could follow a rapid speaker with tolerable

accuracy. And thus he entered upon that strange, and
to most young men very pleasing life of daily journalism.

Pleasing, because it sets at defiance all the carefully-in-
stilled rules of commonplace life; because here the young
man lives, so to speak, among his antipodes: sleeps when
others wake, works when others rest, plays when others
work; because his very labors have in them all the excitement and chance of a game; because his success, if
he is successful, is at once declared, his failure quickly
decided; because he makes his own opportunities, may
give fullest rein to his enterprise, and has his ambition
strung to its highest by the consciousness that each day
will bring his reward for the shrewd and faithful service
of yesterday. Better even than the sea is this life to an
adventurous young man; for here is all the chance of the
sailor's life, ten times its opportunities, and none of its
monotony. He wakes, not knowing when or where he
shall next sleep. He eats wherever hunger may seize
him; smokes whenever the humor strikes; may go anywhere and everywhere; and has—last and best of all to
the fresh tastes of youth—the delicious privilege of re-
versing that stupid proverb which speaks of "early to
bed and early to rise": for your reporter's maxim is,
that nothing happens before half past eleven A.M., and he
makes it a point to breakfast in bed at ten.

To collect facts, in these days of Stoffle's novitiate,
seemed to him the very noblest and most delightful employment for the human soul and body. It had all the
odd charm of walking along the sea-beach finding shells;

only here was not the tiresome uniformity of the shore. A reporter is a kind of roving detective on the search for stray information; a Bow Street officer in pursuit of runaway items; a flibustier diligently capturing the rich argosies of news which fall in his way. To gather facts: that is the great aim of his life. No matter what, no matter where, no matter how; for to a reporter a fact is a fact—and I am sorry to say that to some of the craft a fiction, if it only savor of blood and thunder, is also a fact. To him an Item is the one thing worth living for. He looks on the world only as a vast manufactory of Items; on men as the drudges who by painful labors produce Items for him; on the newspaper as the noble repository of the Items he collects. He regards events only from the historical point of view. A murder is an Item. A fire is an Item. A war is a vast and delicious collection of Items. Where the accident is there are the reporters; and when his train is smashed up, or his steamboat bursts her boiler, he emerges from the ruins pencil in hand, and hails the first passing wagon to bear an Item to "the office."

It is not strange that a young man, fresh from a country college, with the constitution of a horse, the stomach of a jackass (quite capable of digesting the toughest thistles provided by dubious eating-houses), and a healthy love of adventure and variety, becomes an enthusiastic and therefore an expert reporter.

But there is a certain danger in this enthusiasm. A mere collector of facts is a melancholy object. For a fact is not only a stubborn thing; it is a stupid, dead, inani-

mate, worthless piece of carrion, which lies there, supine,
till some one comes and breathes a soul of meaning into
it.   Thus I might call a reporter a resurrectionist, prowl-
ing about for such corpse-like facts; and the danger is,
that this enthusiastic body-snatcher shall by and by become a mere ghoul, subsisting contentedly on the dead
carrion he resurrects.   God does not permit men (nor
nations) to stand still; and this man whom I have called
detective, flibustier, resurrectionist, must either become
an intelligent being, appreciating the value and signifi-
cance of his facts, and thus prepared to infuse into them
the breath of life and reason, or else he becomes a mere
vampire, fattening on the gross carrion which he daily
disentombs from the grave of events.

If we were all sensible men, with abundant leisure, we
might perhaps dispense with the editor, and ourselves digest the crude food of news which makes up the staple
of a daily paper.   But life is short and dollars are scarce;
and as we necessarily take our facts at second-hand from
the reporter, so we are obliged, in most cases, to take their
interpretation at second-hand also.   For you and I, dear
reader—I, who am puzzling my brains all day over my
shears and my accounts, and you who perhaps have no
brains to puzzle—have not time, not to speak of ability,
to work out the problem which the news columns present
to us every morning.

Here comes in the editor—the interpreter.

The reporter may be a Gradgrind, but the editor must
be a prophet.   The reporter need only be an intelligent
machine; the editor must be an intelligent man.   In fact,

he ought to be the most able and the most honest man in the community. Perhaps he is.

Who reads the tedious columns of twaddle headed "Proceedings in Congress?" Surely no sensible man voluntarily stupefies himself with such stuff, which is not ordinarily fit even to put a man pleasantly to sleep. I know it is a great and glorious piece of enterprise to give three columns of it every morning; but I gladly pay two cents for the *Daily Golden Egg* because I know that my friend Goose will in three lines give me a full and correct summary of the three columns, while in a quarter of an hour I can know, from his editorial report, what is the sum and sense of all that has happened in the world for the last twenty-four hours, and am thus able to go to my daily duties in the shop, not only stuffed with news, but bristling with opinions.

This is the use of an editor; and as Stoffle is now to be advanced to this important post of manufacturer of opinions, of judge, in fact, of "what is best," we come naturally to the fourth division of this biography:

IV.—IN WHICH "SIMON SAYS WIGGLE-WAGGLE."

Before a man can manufacture opinions he should have a few of his own; just as when my wife wants her hens to lay, she carefully supplies a few nest eggs of finest white chalk. Now whatever our young men get at college, they seldom get opinions. It might be thought that institutions for the training of youth would naturally communicate something of this kind; but opinions, unfortunately, are thought mischievous, and "eminently to be avoided;" and by the time a man gets thoroughly imbued with the great truth that twice two makes four, he is commonly turned out on the world, labelled "graduate." You get (and forget) Latin, and Greek, and mathematics; and when you are done with that you get a sheep-skin; and being thrust out into the world, find that the only really useful part of your training is some such stray accomplishment as short-hand, which you have trifled with in your uncertain hours of ease.

Stoffle was for some three years an enthusiastic collector of facts before he had a passable knowledge of their value. But when this came about he found himself one day disgusted with his profession.

Most men take to letters from a desire to make a figure in the world; and though the result is, in the majority of cases, only a conspicuous 0, out of every thousand who use the pen one or two also use their brains; and of these a few become able editors. Now when Stoffle's enthusiasm began to cool off, when the Item was beheld in its natural state, and ceased to be in apotheosis, he began to fear that his figure also was to be a small one; and therefore to bestir himself with a healthful discontent. Three years pass very quickly, especially to a man who works hard and likes his work. But at twenty-five the world looks differently than at twenty-two; and at twenty-five Stoffle, who had come to town a simple-hearted country youth, with no particular hopes, except for a speedy wedding and a plain cottage in the country, beheld himself a man with a career before him, a man with possibilities. Now a dinner of herbs, with love, is very good; but a stalled ox has its temptations also, to people who are not confirmed vegetarians. And in that middle passage in life, when young men are vibrating between love and ambition, it occurs, not unreasonably, to many a one, why not "better a stalled ox with love?"

Or if not both, then which?

As Stoffle, now rid of reporter's cares, and writing himself Editor, began to see more and more of those splendid possibilities which men call a career, I am sorry to say the fervor of his affection for poor Lucy Jones declined. At first it was of course impossible to marry; and by the time it became barely possible, it was also become barely possible to Stoffle to put it off. As his life grew larger, and its scope broader, the passion which had absorbed him while at college, and which, like most other young men, he had regarded not only as the noblest, but as the only noble one, began to be overshadowed by others. Love and ambition are to each other as heat and cold.

When Stoffle's fairly roused ambition had once clearly opened his eyes, he saw that the world is only a foolish world, anxious to be ruled; and that it requires no vast wisdom or goodness to rule it, but only a certain strength of will, a certain thickness of skin, a certain readiness of speech. For this foolish world, like children frightened in the dark, insists on being talked to, and is greatly more particular about the sound than the sense. It is not absolutely necessary that you see the road, to guide your

fellows, if only you boldly say that you see it; and if
you want to be a very great statesman or a very able editor, your most useful quality may be the unscrupulous
shrewdness of a special pleader. Now when Stoffle per-
ceived all the splendid possibilities in the life of a man
who has gained such an insight as this at twenty-five, I
do not wonder that the stalled ox quite concealed from
his view that dinner of herbs which is the ideal of under-
graduate philosophers.

Meantime Lucy, who had unluckily no career open to
her, sat at home, like a good, affectionate creature, glory-
ing in the success of her lover, and prizing him the more
highly as she became aware that he was like to prove
himself a man among men. She, too, was content to
wait, almost as content as Stoffle; for she, too, had her
ambition, what right-minded woman has not? Only a
woman's ambition contains in solution so very little of
the acid of selfishness that it does not corrode her love.

The difference between reporter and editor is quite as
great as that between a pickpocket and a highwayman,
or between a resurrectionist and a professor of anatomy.
The reporter is a Bohemian, a lounger, a rough stick;
tolerated but not recognized by society; admitted official-
ly to write the bulletins of fashion, but ignored person-
ally, or at best consigned to the doubtful company of the
awkward squad. But the editor is a man of social and
political standing. Lord Palmerston says he is glad to
invite him to his house—not as editor, but as gentleman—the dear, blarneying old joker! and the Fifth
Avenue, and every other avenue (if there are any oth-

ers), is open to him, with us. With such a new life necessarily come in new wants, new hopes, new desires, new aims. A caterpillar feeds contentedly on its cabbage-leaf, happy if it has secured the sunny side of its limited world. But a butterfly! Think of a Prometheus glued to a cabbage-leaf!

It is not wonderful, then, that in this new sphere to which Stoffle was now translated he should desire to shape his life according to the new lights in which he walked; and that, among other changes, the thought of poor country-bred Lucy became presently somewhat distasteful to this enlightened young fellow. Why should a man marry? Was it necessary? Was it best? Especially a young man with a career opening to him? Not only this, but how would the world, his new world, look upon this country girl? How fatally ill-matched would this rising young man of society be with a girl who probably could not cross a floor! This already-admired wit, with a wife who had no more conception of a sarcasm than a post! What would his friends say? Should he throw his best chances away? Single-handed, he felt it in him to conquer this, his new world. Should he clog his arms and disable himself for a contest in which his whole soul was enlisted?

Oh weary questions, which men ask themselves when they have already decided! Oh foolish words, with which men seek to hide what they dare not face!

And yet, plead as you may, face it you must. And after all it is a question not so easy to decide—this one. What shall a man do, finding himself so placed, bound

with such bonds, and hoping such hopes? Men grow;
hopes, fears, and loves do change. As we advance the
horizon widens, and that which but yesterday we thought
the utmost boundary and very gate of heaven, seems now
but a poor fleeting cloud; and beyond another heaven
opens to our longing eyes.

And the cloud?

If you are a determined man, like Stoffle, you sail
through it, looking neither to right nor left, but only
straight forward.

It was wisely written that once in every man's life he
is taken into a high mountain, and there tempted. It
was not altogether inexcusable in Stoffle, perhaps, if on
this occasion he mistook his conscience to be the Devil,
and looking the awful shape resolutely in the face, wrote
to Miss Jones that "he could not reconcile it to his
sense of right to marry without love; and therefore felt
it a duty, no less to her than to himself, to own that his
feelings toward her had for some time undergone a serious change. While the esteem he had for her character
and her virtues was in nowise diminished, he was constrained to confess that his affections were no longer enlisted. He found himself so entirely swallowed up in his
business life, and so constrained by its necessities, that in-
voluntarily he had ceased to look forward to marriage
with that happy anticipation and content which, in his
opinion, every one should bring to this, the most important step in life. In fact, it seemed to him that men of
his profession should, if possible, avoid marriage. In
such a case he felt it would be doing Miss Jones the sad-

dest wrong to ask her to become his wife; and though he felt bound to her by his plighted word, and held himself in readiness to fulfill that word, yet a desire for her happiness, much more than his own, convinced him of the propriety of dissolving those promises to the fulfillment of which he had once looked forward with such true pleasure. If Miss Jones should agree with his views he begged that she would signify it by returning him his letters; and he remained ever her most obedient servant."

And receiving his letters by return of mail, with only "Good-bye" written on the little slip of white paper which wrapped them, Stoffle, feeling less elated than he had anticipated, shook himself, and was free.

Perhaps the angry reader will say he was a rascal. I do not intend to argue the point, though I have heard a good deal said on both sides. It is one of those disputed questions in which it is not easy to decide what is best, and which therefore no prudent story writer ought to discuss.

Nevertheless, have patience, O angry reader! Do not judge too harshly: it is not given to every man to believe in God.

And then, consider: is it exactly fair for the young ladies of a college town to take snap-judgment on the susceptible hearts of the collegians? What right have they to let themselves be courted and won by men who only think love the best thing because they have as yet no knowledge of any thing but love and Latin, between which 'tis easy enough to choose; who are ambitious to win love, because they know of nothing else they can win? How evidently unfair to take advantage of these inexperienced youth!

And again: The desire of reward is one of the noblest and most useful of human instincts. "What shall we do to be saved?" is the question of most import in the world; and even here the thought of reward vastly overshadows and almost annihilates any consideration of pleasure in the service. The laborer is worthy of his hire; and when a man, be he editor or stone-breaker, does a fair day's work, it is because he wants a fair day's wages. To be sure, the old Divines insisted that we should "cultivate a willingness to be damned." But the world has changed since then; and even the good Samaritan nowadays has a price for his oil, and slips his business card into the vest-pocket of the wounded traveller. Callow youth prates loudly of "disinterestedness" in public men; but I dare say his Excellency the President could tell another story; and, indeed, when you look into the Decalogue, surely the most charming commandments are those "with promise." If you say this is wrong, you make a serious blunder, for even God holds out everywhere a hope of reward, as where it is written "Honor thy father and mother, that thy days may be long in the land." To be sure he did not add, be an able editor or ardent politician that thy fame may fill the land, and thy pockets empty the treasury. But yet, the greater the wages the better the service; and when you call a man rascal, because he hesitates to give up the only wages he values, and tie down his life to a narrow round of virtuous but prosaic duties, it only shows that you have not yourself had the option. It is only smart fishermen who are tempted to fish on Sundays. Your blockhead, who catches no fish at any time, does not grudge the tedious day which sees his craft anchored in Sabbath rest.

The question which presented itself to Stoffle in this crisis of his life, was whether, for a mere point of honor, he should spoil his career. Floating on that "tide, which taken at the flood leads on to fortune," whether he should run into an obscure wayside bay and permanently beach his vessel. Peering into that future, which has such a glorious brightness at twenty-five, Stoffle saw —or thought he saw—himself standing at the junction of two roads, one leading to marriage, obscurity, and a life-long struggle for bread and butter; the other leading to fame, power, position, and wealth. On one side was only a weary, never-ceasing strife between duty and inclination, in which duty must ever have the upper hand; on the other, the best opportunity for the fullest development of his intellectual powers, and an adequate reward for labors which were a delight in themselves.

What is best in such a case as this every man must decide for himself. Being the man he was, Stoffle decided that a scruple should not stand between him and his brightest future. Let him that is without sin cast the first stone.

It is not given to every man to believe in God. It is not in vain that so many commandments are with promise; and perhaps he is wisest who takes God at his word.

There is a divinely-instituted " division of labor" which far-sighted people are apt to overlook. " Paul may plant, and Apollos water, but God giveth the increase."

Now Stoffle intended to fulfill all these offices himself.

A man's career is like a ship under full sail : the wind drives her unceasingly, and it remains only for the helmsman to elect his course and trim his sails. When once Stoffle saw himself clear of that lee-shore on which he had feared to strand his dearest hopes, and with fair winds sailing on the broad sea of editorial life, he did not fail to carry on sail. He was willing to "pay labor" for power, as Dr. Johnson says of Sir Thomas Browne. Day and night he toiled to fit himself more and more for that position of able editor which seemed to him, as it seemed to the Reverend Doctor Wiseacre, the very highest to which a man might in these days aspire. An editor should be the most intelligent man in the community— and he would be that. And the most honest? Well, yes : but what is honesty? You say what you believe ; but suppose you do not believe in any thing? The able editor should be the chiefest statesman of the State. But even statesmen are mortal ; and when the question has once occurred to a mortal man, whether it is best to do right, something depends on the answer he gives it. One thing is certain—this question must be categorically answered. Simon may say wiggle-waggle, but Fate says, in her sternest tones, "Yes or no, and stick to it." Now, when this able editor had said " No " to poor Lucy, whom he regarded just then as the inscrutable Fate, there was no return. He had burned his ships, and henceforth his course was onward.

It is a question which embarrasses men more the higher they stand, this one whether it is best to do right. I am quite sure that honesty is the best policy for my porter and clerks. But for myself? Think of a tailor without cabbage! And a fashionable tailor too, that unfortunate who has to lose many a heavy bill to gain the countenance of the fine world; and who must somehow make it up, you know: for even a tailor must live, and if he is given to scribbling, as I am, so much the worse the chance.

Stoffle was no fool; but a man of large intellect, of broad views, and growing culture. What knowledge bore on his part in life he diligently acquired. History, politics, finance, geography, commerce, were things so faithfully studied that no event could turn up but he had a precedent at his pen's point; no strange complication but he found its solution in a stranger of other days.

But of what avail all history, all knowledge, if it yet remains an open question, "What is best?" The life of an able editor is surely the greatest that is lived in these days. Queens, Emperors and Presidents affect the destinies of nations; but this editor has his voice in every struggle that goes on in the world, and sets his pen to every question that agitates our planet. And must he, too, ask "What is best?" And vainly ask? That question which his traditional million of readers put to him every morning over their coffee, how has he struggled with it by gas-light in his dingy editorial box ten hours ago!

Of course *the right* is best, the simple-hearted Doctor Wiseacre would say. But the one lesson which Stoffle's life had hitherto taught him, was that in certain cases the right is not best.

And what then? Why, then comes in statesmanship. Given, that there is no God, given, that this "right" is an orphan going about the world tolerably helpless, and then you have a logical necessity for Statesmen, Diplomatists, Napoleons, and Editors.

And every body knows that the right is not always best.

Whereby men have gained to themselves immortal fame as skillful tinkers, and being lucky, have died on some such lonely shelf as St. Helena, muttering querulous complaints about Grouchy, who did not come up in time.

As though Grouchy ever came up in time.

It is a secret which shrewd men soon learn in our metropolis, that the difference between prosperity and poverty is just the difference between employing and being employed. There came a day when Stoffle, being now an able editor, might exchange his liberal but stated salary, and become proprietor as well as editor. But to do this money was necessary; and for the present he had some fame, but little money. In this crisis of his affairs, when, for a second time, there appeared a serious obstacle in the way to his advancement on that career he had chosen for himself, there came to his aid one of the best and most ingenious inventions of a commercial age. Some enthusiastic writers have labored to prove that women rule in every society; but I aver on the contrary that they have been the sport of every stage of human progress, from barbarism to civilization. In Africa you buy your wife; in Middle-aged Europe you had to fight for her, whereby the number of bachelors was greatly increased; and now Stoffle bartered his reputation and social position for a certain fortune, and was lucky enough to get into the bargain a very pretty wife, whom, if the exigencies of his career had permitted it, he might in a short time have grown to love sincerely and perhaps devotedly.

And Stoffle being thus fortunately married, which every one must acknowledge to be the best thing he could do under the circumstances, we come to another part of this history :

V.—IN WHICH "SIMON SAYS DOWN."

When a man has written about Europe and its affairs for some years, it is surely best that he should see with his own eyes some of the people and countries he has so long exercised his pen about. It might be best, even, to see Europe before you begin to write about it; but the best thing is not always practicable, as every body knows; and one thing is certain, that if Stoffle had foolishly kept his faith with Lucy he might have deluded a credulous public with opinions about European

affairs for a quarter of a century, and even then not seen
with his eyes the nations he had judged. Thus it appears that Lucy was in reality sacrificed for the public
benefit, which, if duly explained to her, would doubtless
have greatly assuaged her grief.

But Lucy was a sensible girl, who did not need this
satisfaction to dry up her tears. I am afraid the angry
reader will be angrier still when I tell him that while
Stoffle MacGurdigan, Esquire, was travelling over Europe, getting new and improved views of what is best,
Lucy was being courted by a worthy professor of the
college whence her former lover had set out on his career; and when Stoffle and his bride were on their home-
ward passage Lucy became the happy and honored wife
.of Professor White. It is a disagreeable thing to mention, and calculated to destroy all one's preconceived and
beautiful ideas of female fidelity and the power of true
love, and all that, this marriage of Lucy's; but it is a
fact which could not well be concealed by a faithful historian; and after all, I have known a number of other
young·ladies do just as Lucy did, and with, I must own,
the happiest consequences. Men, of course, never do
so; and if Mrs. Betsey had jilted me, a very unlikely
thing, as I was thought a good match even before I
knew her, I am sure I should have been a happy bach-
elor to this day. But that is neither here nor there.

. Stoffle came home from Europe, as most of us do,
with a batch of new and improved ideas of what is
best. It is a curious fact that the only Americans who
are troubled with serious doubts about the success of our

great and glorious experiment of a government, are those who have "run through" Europe. These experienced men of the world, who set out on their travels with a large spread-eagle next to their hearts, almost invariably return with a poor opinion of Democratic Institutions, and tell you, confidentially, with a French shrug, and a countenance of dolorous certainty, that "it's of no use, you know; Republics may last for a generation or two— but your only steady wear is a good monarchy." And if you could see a little further into this Jeremiah's thought, you would find behind the good monarchy a comfortable aristocracy, to divide among them the large slices of fat which prosperous monarchies abound in.

You must not blame these drivelers and doubters too much. A run through Europe is not calculated to sharpen the intelligence of every man; and really, to men who live in a chronic hurry, the speedy ways of an Imperial Dictator can not fail to recommend themselves; while it is difficult to imagine a more disheartening spectacle to an ambitious man of intellect, who feels that his knowledge ought to be both power and wealth, than the shabby Swiss confederacy, surrounded as it is by such splendid kingdoms and empires. Stoffle had an uneasy feeling that such laborers as he were worthy of a greater hire than is provided for with us; and I admit freely that to a laborer who looks only to his hire our greatest prizes even must seem not only very little, but very hard to get at, which is precisely what the fox, had he been honest, would have said of the grapes.

Stoffle came back from Europe, convinced that there

are many animals in the world more splendid to look upon, more useful, and perhaps longer lived, than that spread-eagle of which he had in his grass-days been a somewhat blind worshiper. Until you have seen a king or an emperor, it is not unnatural to think highly of the President. But when you have once been permitted to look at the ways, and thoughts, and means of European statesmen, our own politics look so petty, our best men seem so ridiculously, what shall I say, virtuous? that a man who has the soul of a statesman and whose mind can comprehend and delight in the task of keeping the world balanced, can not help a little regret that he was born to no greater work than voting for, or being voted, Member of Congress, and being opposed perhaps by a hotel keeper, or a corner grocery man. Did you ever hear one of these returned Americans utter the word *canaille?* It is true, they do not often pronounce it any thing else than *canael*, but the air with which they mispronounce it is absolutely perfect. It shows that the heart is all right, though the tongue may halt.

Stoffle, who had as contemptuous an opinion of the American eagle as an enlightened traveller need have, was not, however, the man to quarrel with that beloved and somewhat vindictive bird. Like a wise man he made the best of his fate. He was now in the prime and strength of his powers. Long practice had given him a splendid facility in writing, by which his stores of facts were brought to bear upon the various questions of the day with an ability which was undeniable. He had wit; he had logic; he had knowledge; he had experience; he had tact. He was untiring, energetic, pertinacious, and ready. And he had one vast advantage over other men, his readers, that he did not believe in any thing but his career. Thus it is not matter for surprise that he was successful. When an able man sets all his powers to one object, he is not likely to be foiled, much less if that object is his own advancement.

Thus Stoffle was at last the ideal of able editors; and now honors crowded upon him, and riches; he was not only a public writer but also a public speaker; and at last the final tribute which Yankee curiosity pays to Yankee notoriety or fame, was rendered also to him: he was invited to lecture. Among other invitations came one from the students of his college, who, remembering that this eminent man had once studied within their walls, asked him to speak to them also the words of wisdom with which he was surcharged.

Great as Stoffle had come to be, you are to understand that he had yet a heart in his bosom; and the perusal of this note of invitation, " written by permission of the Reverend Doctor Wiseacre," and signed by the Faculty as well as the committee of students, drew his thoughts back to the dear simple old school-days which he had not very often remembered in these busy later years. For a little while he lived the old life over again, with all its hopes, and fears, and loves; which, looking back upon them now, from his proud eminence, seemed to him so curiously trivial. "Poor Lucy!" he sighed, as her soft voice resounded dimly over that dead past; and then remembered with a smile which was nearly a laugh, that amusing lecture on the Daily Press, which the old Doctor had delivered to Lucy and himself one evening, so many centuries ago.

"What a singular fossil a College President gets to be!" he smiled to himself, knocking the white ash from the end of a mild Cabaña. "He was right in his advice to me, by good luck; but how odd! How it would astonish the old cock to show him the reality of which he sees only the beautiful but impossible shadow! But he wouldn't believe me."

He prepared himself carefully for his appearance before the College audience. They had no votes for him, to be sure; but he felt more solicitous to gain honor here than almost aught elsewhere, here, where something told him he deserved it less. The lecture had for its subject the glories of free government; and in it he took occasion to speak gratefully of their venerable and honored President, to whose sound instruction and sage advice he owed it, he was pleased to say, that, starting in life as a poor friendless youth, without any advantages which might not be obtained by any poor man's son, he now stood before them what he was. Nothing touches an American audience so sensibly as this now tolerably stale twaddle about self-made men. They do not see that, in this country, to be born poor is to enter the race unencumbered, and that in truth it is far more difficult for a rich American's son to acquire useful knowledge, energy, and tact, than to crawl through the eye of a needle. Let us hope that some day this humbug of struggling poverty and work ending triumphantly in a brown-stone front on the Fifth

Avenue will also be exploded; and that we shall cease to count our victories by the dollar's worth.

Lucy was among the audience you may be sure. She could not but remember, and with a slight pang from a wound long ago healed over, that this was an occasion to which she had once looked as one of especial pride to herself. And now—

The lecture being done, and properly applauded, the lecturer approached Mrs. Professor White, and congratulating her on her good looks, begged to be introduced to her husband.

Lucy was rather glad when Doctor Wiseacre bore her old-time lover off to his house. It was no small treat for the worthy President, living all his life in retirement, to meet a man fresh from the outer world, and living, so to speak, in the face of affairs. To rub himself against such a brilliant man of the world, was a cheering thing for the dear old fogy, who, though he thought Stoffle as a public man by no means in the right, and sometimes shuddered at what seemed to him very unscrupulous conduct, could not deny him splendid talents, nor himself the credit of having drawn them out.

Sitting cozily by the blazing fire, they rambled back to old times, and at last the President said: "Well, Stoffle, I scarce thought my prophecy about your career would have had so great a fulfilling. I suppose you would not exchange your present honors for the poet's wreath you once longed for?"

"No, indeed," replied Stoffle, emphatically; "that was one of the silly vagaries of my youth, of which I was soon cured when once I came in contact with practical life. Our time has not come yet for poetry, and I hope it never will. There never was a practical poet."

"Perhaps not; and, after all, the greatest poets could not do more than you gentlemen of the press are doing. I don't agree with your views altogether, you know—"

"Why, no; but I think that is because you mistake the whole scope of journalism," interrupted Stoffle, determined now to give this old fogy a shot. "You are not practical. I remember, as though it were yesterday, that fine speech of yours about the daily paper. But I assure you you are very much mistaken. It is an error to suppose that a daily journal has a mission any more than any other commercial enterprise. One man sells cotton, and another man sells newspapers, and it is the business of each to be successful, that is to say, to gain the best profit he can from his investment. Each alike brings to his undertaking a certain capital, and a certain amount of business talent, experience, and shrewdness. Every merchant has his public, whom he is obliged to please, or fail. A sensible merchant, who desires to keep out of the bankruptcy court, will, of course, strive to make his public as numerous as possible. · At the same time no merchant's public is so exacting and capricious as ours, because none needs to be so large; and therefore to carry on a newspaper successfully requires perhaps, though I say it, more talent and tact and energy and shrewdness than any other business in the world.

"The first business of a daily journal is to give news,

all the news, more news, if possible, than any other paper gives, and of a more attractive kind. This is the prime necessity, before which every thing else pales. Of course it must happen occasionally that I am forced to publish something which, could I afford it, I would not print; and, more frequently, I am obliged to magnify rumors to-day only to contradict them to-morrow; and these things are not pleasant to an editor who desires also to be a gentleman. But what is an unfortunate man to do? There must be newspapers, because the public needs them; and if I do not publish a certain statement some one else will, and my readers go off to another paper. Our public gives us no choice. It is our master. If I do not please it I lose it; if I do not keep up my circulation my advertising fails, and then I sink money, and presently come to a wind up, just as a dry-goods man would who should fail to keep such goods as his lady customers wish. You look sober, Sir; but are we to be less wise than A. T. Stewart?

"Then you spoke of shaping public opinion. You never were more mistaken. An able daily appears to shape public opinion, but it only leads it. The man who has the loudest lungs in a crowd can lead it if he will; but he can not lead it away from its purpose. He can only place himself skillfully at its head, and, knowing its aims, submit to be pushed on in advance. Now a party in the State is only a larger mob. There are always at least two parties; and it is the able editor's first business to ascertain which of the two is the most likely to win, and to lead that. For the biggest crowd is the majority, and

the majority rules, and it the able daily is therefore bound
to lead.

"How about principle, did you say? Don't you see
that there is no principle involved in party warfare?
Certain men want power, are ambitious to rule the nation. They set the people by the ears about an abstrac-
tion, persuade the nation that all depends upon the success of this or that man; and thus play the game of politics. Show me one man of them that has any real principle of action other than that very important one of You
tickle me and I'll tickle you. There is no right or principle involved, and if there was it wouldn't matter; for,
after all our squabbles, God overrules it all for the best.

"It is an editor's business to know what the public
likes, and to give them that. It is a shrewd editor's business to foresee in what direction public opinion is next
to turn, and to be the first to sound the advance in this
new direction. And it is his first duty, when he has by
unwise haste taken a wrong step, to take it back. Ignorant people cry down the London *Times* because, having
yesterday blown hot, to-day it blows cold on the same
subject. But therein lies the secret of its immense success. Yesterday it made a mistake. Before night that
mistake was seen. This morning it comes out with an
able article which appears, but only appears, to shape the
public opinion. In fact, it only gives it voice; and this,
so far as the editorial department is concerned, is the
true course of the daily newspaper—to furnish words
for the ideas which rest dormant and inarticulate in the
minds of the public.

"Conscience, do you say? But, my dear Sir, conscience has nothing to do with it. Don't you see that
plainly enough? Of course we all want to do what is
right. But a newspaper is not a moral agent; it is a
commercial speculation, whose only duty is success. A
dry-goods man would be thought insane who should in-
sist on selling goods which only a few of the community
want. And just in the same way a newspaper aims to
get as large a public as possible. If that public is vacil-
lating, if its moral sense is low, if it cares little for principle and much for interest, that is a misfortune, to be
sure; but the newspaper is not responsible for it. It has
only to follow. It is useless to set yourself to impracticable things. In this world twice two makes four, and
that is a principle we can't change. I do not say that
an editor is not to have opinions of his own. God for-
bid! He can not help having them; and the abler he
is the more unpractical and impracticable his private
opinions are likely to be. Now it is his first duty to be
practical. And if an editor is not successful, what is the
use of him? can you tell me that, Sir? He had much
better saw wood.

"You think the public sensible, and in the main right.
The public is an ass, and can kick. You, simple-hearted
and right-minded country gentleman, think I do not
know what the public wants. But is not my paper successful? and is not that the only criterion? You object to scandal; but I, who do not like it either, know
that the paper which gives the most will sell best. You
think an editor should be governed by high moral prin-

ciple. He ought not to be such an ass as to let any body else use him—that I grant you. But the public does not care for principle. It is a pig, and likes to have its ribs tickled. Let the news be exciting, and it cares not if it be also true. Let the article be slashing, and it matters little whom it slashes. Let the story be strong enough, and you will see that every man has read it, by the fierceness with which every man abuses the paper that gives it."

There was a long silence when Stoffle was done. Each sat gazing into the fire, and busy with his own thoughts. The old president looked grieved and a good deal surprised at the doctrine which his scholar had just laid down to him. Stoffle was so plausible that even a president and doctor of divinity may be excused for asking himself if this was indeed the truth of the matter.

At last the Reverend Doctor Wiseacre looked up into Stoffle's flushed face, and said, "I am sorry I advised you to go to New York."

"And I," said the editor, bowing gracefully, "shall never cease to be grateful for your sound counsel."

"Some day you will think differently. Aaron was not the last high-priest who set up a golden calf for his people to worship, crying, 'These be your gods, O Israel!' But Aaron repented, and so I trust will you. 'Except the Lord build the house, they labor in vain that build it: except the Lord keep the city, the watchman waketh but in vain. It is in vain for you to rise up early, to sit up late, to eat the bread of sorrows: for so he giveth his beloved sleep.'"

" That is all very true," replied Stoffle; "but don't you see you are not practical, my dear Sir; you are not practical."

Saying which he rose to retire; and here I propose to leave him. The historian should be judge and not advocate. It is for him to state the case fairly and trust the verdict to the jury of readers, each of whom must at last settle this question for himself, of " What is best? "

A STRUGGLE FOR LIFE.

A STRUGGLE FOR LIFE.

I.

IT was the last day of the Indiana Conference. All business was dispatched, and the assembled preachers waited only for that last and most important announcement which should decide for each the scene of his next year's labors. In the Methodist communion the bishop who presides over the annual meeting called the "Conference" wields the appointing power. His word, in this matter, has been wisely made supreme; and though, with the degenerating Methodists of the Eastern States, the body of presiding elders prompts the wisdom of their superior, while the larger and wealthier congregations go one step further and ask privately beforehand for the man of their choice, in the generous West they stick to the primitive mode, trusting to the experience of the bishop that he shall so fit the men to the churches that neither may be wronged.

Nor, let it be said here to the honor of those venerable men, who have now for more than half a century exercised this somewhat arbitrary power, has there often been found just cause of complaint.

The list of appointments is prepared during the session of Conference, and is kept strictly secret; so that no one knew, nor could form even a probable guess at his fate. The murmur of voices was therefore hushed, and all listened as with one ear when the bishop rose to solve their riddles for them.

One by one the willing servants bowed their accepting heads, with a sigh of relief or sorrow, and lost their general curiosity in their particular interest. Presently was read out:

"SHOTTOVER STATION: PAUL CLIFTON."

Whereat a few of the elder brethren looked over toward the young man so named, scrutinizing him with critical eyes, as though measuring his fitness for this "Shottover Station;" while others, the younger preachers, looked up with eyes in which pity for him was mingled with unconcealed joy at their own escape.

For they were hard cases at Shottover Station. The Church was small and weak; the "outsiders" a turbulent set, irreverent to the last degree, exceedingly sharp at discovering the preacher's weak points, and very ready to take advantage of them. A very stronghold of Satan was Shottover, where the poor minister need hope for but small pay and less respect, and might think himself lucky if he got off with whole bones. Once or twice, indeed, in years past, they had driven the newly-appointed man away by force of their brawny arms and leathery lungs; and once, taking an exceeding dislike to a young fellow just from college, and serving here his first year (and who, as they complained, "knew every thing"), they had combined together and literally starved him out.

Therefore Shottover was a place to be avoided by all means; a plague-spot which had driven several timid men into other Conferences; and to which now for some years the youngest member was, by general agreement of the bishop with his subordinates, sent to make trial of his budding powers, just as boys who have run away from home to sea are on their first voyage placed in charge of the sky-sails and royal studding-sails, to loose and furl them: whereby at least those whose romance lies but skin-deep, and who were perhaps called, but not chosen, grow to hate the glorious sea-life in the precise proportion as they scrape the skin off their tender shins; and are glad, at the first port, to run away home again.

This I take to be a fine example of Mr. Darwin's recently-advanced theory of "Natural Selection."

Paul Clifton, who sat in pleased unconsciousness a little on one side of the room, like a young bear, all his sorrows before him, was a recent acquisition to the Conference. He had been graduated with honor two years before at a Theological Institute in the East; had preached experimentally, and very acceptably, on various occasions, and to different city and country congregations; had "taken a run over to Europe," and was now counted a promising young man, whom any Conference would be glad to receive; when lo! to the surprise and disappoint-

E

ment of his friends, he set his face Westward, and eschew-
ing the flesh-pots of New York, resolutely wandered into
the desert of Indiana. Another John Baptist, said Miss
Thomasina Dobbs, a romantic young lady, who was
shrewdly suspected of designs upon the reverend Paul's
heart; though very unlike John Baptist indeed, thought
the rough Hoosier preachers, when they saw him pull off
his neatly-fitting kid gloves on coming into the Conference room, and spread a white and clean pocket-hand-
kerchief on the dirty floor whereon to kneel at prayers.

The fact is, young Clifton had been bred in ease, and
had the outside of a gentleman, which is a disadvantage
sometimes: particularly if the inside does not correspond.
He had a young man's natural longing to go out into the
world, and see a little of the rough side of it, to try his
own wings, which he had now for some years been impatiently fluttering on the edge of the paternal nest. Add
to this the honest enthusiasm of a young fellow who be-
lieves himself called to show the heavenly road—not as a
finger-post, as Jean Paul suggests, which only points the
way, but does not move itself. And this tempered, perhaps, by the modest thought that it would be easier for
him, a young and inexperienced man, to lead rough
Hoosiers up this steep and narrow path than the more
refined and intellectual congregations of the East, a little mistake I have known wiser men than the reverend
Paul to make: as though the wildest horses did not need
the most skillful drivers. Put these together, and you
have, I suppose, nearly the mixture of motives which
brought him to avoid the soft ease of a "first-class city

appointment," and join himself to this unknown future of the backwoods.

The bishop regarded him with mild pity as he read him his fate. A set custom could not be violated on his account; nor, indeed, did the venerable man believe that this trial had best be spared the young preacher. When the last hymn was sung, and the prayer and benediction had dismissed the members to their homes, he walked over to where Clifton sat, and shaking his hand encouragingly, said—

"Keep up your spirits, Brother Paul! the sword of the Lord is on your side—'the sword of the Lord and of Gideon.'"

"Yes, yes," remarked an old fellow who overheard these words: "I wish there was a little more Gideon though;" while a hard-featured circuit-rider growled to himself, "'Tain't right, hardly. I've a mind to change places with him; he looks like a good young fellow."

"You leave him alone," interrupted old Father Sawyer; "probably the bishop knows what he's about. Let the young man take his chance. The Lord will provide."

"I don't believe the Lord knows much about Shottover," retorted the circuit-rider, who had enough of Gideon about him, at any rate; and who probably would have enjoyed a tussle with that devil of mischief who was said to be so strongly intrenched in Paul Clifton's new station.

In this regard he differed much from Paul, who was not what you would call a muscular Christian, forcing

people heavenward by the fear of the Lord and a big
fist; but eminently a mild-mannered man, slender, and
more given to his Greek Testament than to his dumb-
bells. Old Peter Cartwright would have counted him
but small potatoes. But then, even Peter is mortal; in
fact, I find nothing so very mortal as muscle.

That he might properly prepare himself for personal
contest with the sons of Belial who made Shottover a
by-word and reproach in the mouths of the brethren,
these took care to fully inform Brother Paul of the various disagreeables and trials he might expect in his new
station. Just in this way my grandmother used to describe to me beforehand, and with great minuteness and
conscientiousness, the nauseous horrors of that inimitable
flavor of disgust, an impending dose of castor-oil. From
which resulted to me, in the end, a strong dislike, not so
much of castor-oil as of grandmothers, and particularly
those of the male sex. Thus advised, and in no very
sanguine temper, Paul rode into Shottover on top of the
stage, on a Saturday morning; and after refreshing his
inner and outward man at the tavern, proceeded to view
his church.

Now, to an earnest and unsophisticated Christian like
the Reverend Paul Clifton, used all his life to the com-
fortably-cushioned pews, carpeted aisles, sofa'd pulpits,
and scrupulous cleanliness of our city churches, the little
meeting-house of Shottover was like to be a shock.

A shock, certainly, to his sense of comfort and decen-
cy; perhaps, who knows? to his faith in the Christian
doctrine.

It is unpleasantly situated in the extreme edge of a bare and sterile clay-bank, down which, I believe, it will slip some rainy day. Its low roof; its mud-be-spattered walls, once painted a dirty white; its narrow door-way, making no allowance for sinners in crinoline; its ragged wagon-shed, like Jack Straw's house, neither wind-tight nor water-tight, and through whose board-sides several generations of idle horses had gnawed sundry holes, which gave their successors occasional privileged squints into a cool meadow beyond, thus pointing a Sunday lesson even to obstinate horse-flesh, by this pleasant vision of heavenly grass fields; and this flanked by an appalling architectural novelty, a bell-tower, or embryo steeple, standing on its own base, and giving the impression to an unfamiliar eye that it had been lifted down from its proper place on the roof by some light-handed giant: all this does not promise well to a man who holds his faith by the ties of mere use and comfort.

Within, the narrow aisles are covered with a fine coating of yellow Indiana mud. The hard, straight-backed, uncushioned pews afford no rest to the wicked; nor indeed to the pious either, unless, as is sometimes the case, piety and fat are found in the same body. The preaching-stand has at least the merit of consistency, being neither cleaner nor more ornamental than the rest of the church. Rain-stained windows; bare, white-washed, and partly "peeled" walls, white where no stains of tobacco betoken the resting-place of some saint who chews the cud of Virginia content beneath the shadow of the preacher's long arms; and a huge stove, whose

two diverging pipes stretch like vast arms along the ceil-
ing on both sides, as though preparing to shed a fervid
blessing on the assemblage : truly here was found cause
sufficient for a series of shocks to Christians of weak faith
or sensitive nerves.

II.

Nevertheless, though cleanliness is next to godliness,
a dirty shirt is not evidence of the unpardonable sin ;
and I have known men whose hard hands and soiled
clothes hid a soul so clean that, if you were not wretchedly near-sighted, and could see at all through a coating
of clean dirt, you at once took such to your heart.

Such an one was Farmer Leighton. A tall, raw-boned,
hard-featured man, with the awkward straddling gait,
uncertain poise of body, and splay feet, which are the rewards an inscrutable Providence decrees for a life of se-
vere toil, perhaps to teach us to look beneath the surface for the truest worth ; perhaps also to warn us that
man does not live by bread alone, and that Mary did indeed choose a better part than serviceable Martha.

Farmer Leighton was now a well-to-do personage in
his little world. A man of some forty-five summers, in
most of which corn-planting, hay-making, reaping, and
housing crops, the multifarious, never-ceasing toils of
the farm, had left their marks not lightly upon him ;
with scant, grizzled side-whiskers, and a chin wretchedly
shaven by a dull razor and an unsteady, wearied hand ;
hair of that tawny sandy hue which betokens several

generations of rough struggle with forest-life, hanging down in straight and tangled locks about his ears and coat-collar; and a Sunday suit of blue Kentucky-jeans, home-made, and ingeniously contrived to show every angle and rough knot and ungraceful line in the poor, ill-used body beneath. This was the man whose harsh, cracked voice, with a querulous quaver in it at first, and a strange after-tone of protecting and loving care, called out

"Now, then, old lady!"

At which a bright bay mare, harnessed to a mud-splashed buggy, standing near the hitching-post at the gate, pricked up her ears and wondered what she had done now.

As though there were no other old lady in the world!

"In a minute," answered a voice from within-doors, having in it also a certain uncertain tremble—a quaver, however, which stood for the fearfulness of a long and much-loving heart, whose meek habit was to fit its motions to the convenience of others; a voice soft and agreeable, even though it was cracked; and hinting of many cares and much housewifely forecast. And presently appeared in the covered way of the comfortable double log-cabin a portly dame to whom this voice belonged.

Her followed a young girl, blue-eyed and fair-haired, as they are in Indiana, and of such buxom and shapely form, combining strength with grace, as is the natural result of "hog and hominy," plenty of fresh air, and a total lack of servants and other incentives to a lazy life. Her name is Miranda Leighton, for which I am sorry, for I believe she might better have been called by some such honest and plain name as Susan, Jane, or Eliza. But the Hoosier farmers, having little other grandeur to bestow upon their children, are pretty sure to give them grand and outlandish names; and I have a respect for facts, which are stubborn things, but useful in their way.

Miranda unfastened her pony from a rack beneath the wagon-shed, where he had stood under shelter, lucky beast! and leading him up to the horse-block, leaped lightly into the saddle. As she settled herself there, helped by her father's kindly hands, a horseman rode into the open by a turn of the road.

"There's John now," said Mrs. Leighton. "John, come, go to church with us."

"I'm goin'," said he. "Ther's a new minister, ain't thar?"

"Yes; and no tricks now, John," urged his mother, beseechingly.

"No, indeed; we're goin' to listen—see what stuff he's made of. Guess the boys 'll be still enough to-day."

"I'll warrant they'll all be thar," grumbled old man Leighton.

Which was a safe guess; for, next to a circus, nothing draws so large a crowd in an Indiana village as public speaking of any kind; and above all, a new preacher. A talent for oratory is worshiped by all the West; and a man who really has something to say, and knows how to say it as though he believed with all his heart, could not have a more appreciative audience than these rough, plain

Indiana farmers. Nor will you find anywhere sharper or more relentless critics than these. As logical as children, and as impatient of humbug, they are ever ready with a biting word, which pierces to the core of some conscious misstatement, or sophistry which the speaker is not himself taken in by.

So the sister and brother rode off together in advance, while the old folks followed at such leisurely pace as suited the bay mare, who had had her own way so many years that she took it now as a matter of right.

Miranda had just returned from school. In Indiana the boys must work, and their schooling comes, if at all, by fits and starts—as they say lawyers get to heaven. It is theirs to battle with the primal curse from their earliest years, and such learning as they get is picked up at odd times, and chiefly from their Bibles and the agricultural papers. But the girls go to school. For them money is laid by ; and as they grow to young womanhood, poor indeed must be the farmer who does not send his daughter away to boarding-school in some city or larger town, where she has, at any rate, the opportunity to gather such of the ways, and thoughts, and accomplishments of a more finished culture as may assimilate best with her nature. With these advantages the daughter becomes the oracle of the house, cherished by all as a being of a superior kind, and greatly held in awe by younger brothers, who submit, with what grace may be, to her dominion. Miranda, as I said, had just returned from school. The free air and pleasant sunshine of this Sunday morning, and the exhilarating canter of the pony, raised her spirits, and gave her courage to administer a scolding to John, some of whose tricks she had heard of on her return from school at Louisville.

"Don't you see it's very wrong?" she asked, with such a sparkle in her eyes as made it vaguely doubtful to contrite John whether it was nearly so wrong as he had before thought to tie a raccoon under the bench occupied by the young ladies' Bible class in church, where it had scratched and snarled at every pause in the sermon, to the great distress of the young ladies and the intense delight of the boys.

"Don't you see it's wrong?" she repeated. "Didn't mother always tell you to be a good boy; and didn't I always tell you to behave?"

"I'm going to be as good as pie, now you've come back, Sis," said John, turning toward the pleased Miranda a face really expressive of a vast amount of contrition. But alas! as he turned in the saddle a horrifying screech interrupted this charming scene.

"O Lord!" exclaimed John, sliding nimbly off his horse, and making a desperate grab after his coat-tails, from a pocket in one of which presently emerged a good-sized cat, spitting out in evident rage at her treatment, and with eyes sparkling, head down, and tail erect, rushed off into the woods.

There was a dead and ominous silence for the space of twenty interminable seconds.

"Now, JOHN!" at last exclaimed Miranda, very slowly, and with an injured air; "NOW, JOHN!"

And then the little witch could hold her grave face no

longer, but burst out into such a peal of laughter that the pony was at a loss to know what it all meant, while the bay mare hurried up her lagging paces, very much surprised indeed, and anxious to discover the cause of such sudden merriment.

"You BAD, WICKED boy!" exclaimed Miranda, catching a moment's breath, and with it a grave face; but seeing John still standing by his horse, with red face, and hands closely held to his coat-tails, she broke away again into a laugh which the woods were very glad indeed to echo.

"I didn't mean to've sot on her," said John, respectfully, willing to mollify his sister; "guess she ain't hurt much.

"I'll catch her if you like," he added, suddenly, in the hope that an offer of service, of whatever kind, would help him out.

"'Tain't that, you stupid boy, you know very well," laughed Miranda, trying to assume that severity of countenance which she felt the occasion and the offense demanded. "What was the cat doing in your pocket, you dreadful fellow?"

"Can't a feller take his cat to church without you pitchin' into him?" retorted John, in injured tones; and then feeling that defense was worse than useless in his case, and seeing, besides, the bay mare approaching, with father and mother peering curiously at their children, he judged it prudent to remount his horse and ride off at such a pace that he was not likely to be caught. But as he rode Miranda noticed, with a chuckle of satisfaction,

that he still held one hand carefully in the neighborhood
of that coat-pocket which had contained the luckless cat.

III.

The Reverend Paul Clifton rose early on this Sunday
morning, and was the first man—after the sexton—to enter the church.   To say that he felt comfortable would be
to make him out a fool, which he was not.   It was a novel
situation; and I dare say it costs a gentleman more serious thought to preach to a congregation of backwoods-
men than it does Peter Cartwright to expound his Gospel to a Fifth Avenue audience.   When he had seen his
church, or meeting-house, when he had made the acquaintance of the sexton, and some others of the leading
members, when he had slept upon his impressions, and
now, on this bright Sunday morning, was arrived at the
climax of his troubles, the reader who will believe me
that the Reverend Paul was not only an honest young
fellow, but also a man who thought modestly of his own
abilities, will not be surprised that he sat in uncomforta-
ble anxiety for the result.

For to fail here was to fail utterly. I am ashamed to
refer again to Mr. Darwin, but here was what that eminent naturalist very properly calls a "struggle for life."

It was only in these two days that the solemn question, What is the full force and meaning of this office I
have taken upon myself? began to crowd upon him in
all its wide and serious bearings.

And what, indeed, is it to be what we call indifferent-ly preacher, pastor, missionary?

The Natural History of the Clergyman is still to be written. I do not intend to bore the sufficiently impatient reader by interpolating in this place any attempt at so important a work. But pending the advent of the great ecclesiastical Agassiz, what is to prevent me from setting down here my little preliminary "Essay on Classification?" See: there is,

1. The wishy-washy young man, who would starve in any other calling, and therefore literally "preaches for a living;"

2. The fluent young man, who preaches because that is the most impressive way of saying nothing;

3. The ambitious young man, who sees that the prefix Reverend gives, even in our Protestant America, a certain power and influence to its possessor;

4. The wide-awake young man, who knows that for him there is no such easy way to gain bread and butter and honor (and a rich wife) as the pulpit;

5. The studious young man, who turns clergyman that he may gain leisure for his favorite books and studies;

6. The young man who has a certain intellectual theory of Christianity, with which he thinks it desirable to quiet the world. This one, I sometimes think, lacks only a little true piety to be indeed the model clergyman of the age;

And, lastly—not to make this list too long—there is your man who, feeling not only his neighbor's but his own pride, and selfishness, and arrogance, and forgetful-

ness of God, and of all good words and works, feels also
that above all mere dickering for place, or power, or superfluous bread and butter, or any low ambition whatever,
is the divine office of leading his fellows from these
abysses, where devils lie in wait for their souls, to those
green fields where Christ the Shepherd waits his sheep.
To such men he said of old, and says to-day, "Go ye
into all the world and proclaim the Gospel to every creature, beginning at Jerusalem." To such Christ is he
who "came into the world to save sinners, of whom I
am chief." These are they, the true ministers of His
Word, following and teaching Him with that divine love
and charity which compels the rudest souls. Shall we
complain if any such go forth comprehending their great
work vaguely—looking out upon it as through a glass,
darkly? doubting, hesitating, in fear and trembling?
like Gideon, the son of Joash, asking vain signs of their
Lord? I think few men set out on their life-work, if
it be any thing higher than mere selfish toil, with any
clear ideas of what they are to do. Your logical man is
your thorough rascal. So let us not doubt of Paul Clifton, if his heart sank down into his boots as he sat in
his pulpit on that Sunday morning, watching the en-
trance of his congregation; who now began to slide in,
in little awkward squads of six or seven, bashfully ex-
amining "the new minister" as they pushed up the aisles
into their seats.

They need not strain their eyes to see him. Here was
no dim religious light, such as some of our city churches
affect, and which is so admirable a help to sleep that I

don't wonder wearied Wall Street cultivates it. The broad pleasant sunshine poured in boldly through that part of the open and curtainless windows not obstructed by the opaque bodies of sundry Hoosier lads who preferred a seat in the window ledges, a luxury refused them on week-days, when slab-sided Jehoram Baker, the Yankee pedagogue, here taught the young idea how to shoot.

And now as Miranda, her face composed, and her hand holding her brother's arm, marched that reluctant youth up the aisle, her dress caught one of the intellectual pop-guns which lay at random about the floor; whereat a small boy, coming behind with his mother, gave an anxious glance, then dove down desperately into the crowd, crying out in a shrill treble, "Dog-on it, that's my speller!" Then brandished aloft the precious dog's-eared volume he had rescued, and was incontinently suppressed by his irate mother, who looked maternal thunders at the unlucky urchin who had dared to "holler out in meetin'!"

Paul smiled as his eyes took in the scene, whose grotesque humor relieved him for a moment from his load of anxiety. And now the service began.

If you think I am going to give you the sermon, or any part of it, you are mistaken. A mere sermon don't often convert any body, not even the preacher. Old John Wesley augured badly of the man who told him that he, Wesley, had converted him; and begged him to pray the Lord to do it over. Webster defines a sermon to be a pious and instructive discourse. Now, it can't be pious without being instructive; and, moreover, Dr. Webster's definition excludes a considerable class of sermons, which are neither pious nor instructive, but only logical, or theological, which is worse. For I believe, with one of our greatest preachers, that all theology comes of the devil; and when a man gets into his pulpit and begins to lay out the Christian doctrine to me by rule of thumb, or by any other rule but that golden one of which Christ said that he who keeps this fulfills all the law and the prophets—then I try very hard to run my thoughts off on some little side track of my own, where they may quietly take another train and go to a quite different place from the preacher's.

When Paul rose he read aloud those beautiful promises of Christ on the Mount. And as he read, his heart, till now dumb with fear before this strange people, grew strong and full with the dear love which speaks in every line of those blessed words. It is not so much words a speaker needs as thoughts; and not so much thoughts as the one great inspiring thought which shall bind his audience to him, and make him and them from that time kindred and of one spirit. In this sign he conquers. And this sign? Men call it sympathy: He called it love. In what manner should he speak? How should he manage, to please them? had been Paul's troubled thought. But now they were no longer they. No longer farmers, rude, uncouth, peculiar, different—but men and brethren, of the same thoughts, the same hopes, the same fears, the same heaven-born aspirations. Not strangers, but kindred, saved by the same blood, reaping the same promises, tempted in all things, even as was He who suffered all that we might follow him. "Be ye all things to all men," said the Apostle; to whom this command was doubtless plainer than to some of his successors.

Do you think words fail the man whose heart is full to bursting? Words these were of Paul's, neither brilliant, nor fine, nor profound, nor trashy; but very simple indeed. And though this young man had satisfactorily displayed his talents before several cultivated city congregations, this was in truth the first sermon of his which went to his own heart. Do you know what Christ meant when he said to them: "Go ye and preach this gospel to all the nations, *beginning at Jerusalem?*"

Jehoram Baker, the callous Yankee pedagogue, who could stand more hard preaching than any man I ever knew, was cheated of his customary nap that morning. The people were very much surprised. They didn't quite understand it. That is to say—they did. When Paul came among them after service it was not as "the new minister," but as an old friend. He needed no introduction to men and women whose hearts he had touched so nearly. He was one of themselves: no fine city gentleman come to teach rough Hoosiers what they knew perhaps better than he; nor any rude soldier of the Cross, so overwhelming them with the thunder of his Gospel artillery as to leave no hearing for the soft loving voice of the great Captain of our salvation, who wills not the death of sinners—and surely never wished to see them damned before they were dead. Nor, lastly, was he, to their conception, any theological mummy, stiff with the wrappings of old formulas, and with dry husks where live men keep their hearts.

Only a gentleman.

I hope you will not ask to me to say "Christian gentleman;" because then I shall think you don't know what it is to be a gentleman—or a Christian.

And do you think a gentleman can not prevail with such plain folk as these without bluster, and casting away his own true nature? Does not the greater contain the less? And who told you that this old Hoosier farmer, in cowhide boots and homespun clothes, slow of speech and awkward in manner, is not the truest gentleman God ever made?

IV.

"Father says you must come home with us," said Miranda Leighton, pointing to where "Father" stood before the meeting-house door holding the mare, who was restive for her dinner. There were invitations a plenty to "come and stay with us;" but "Squire Leighton" carried the day, and bore off Paul, who found himself presently in a comfortable farm-house, where his host presented him in farmer fashion:

"This is the old lady; this is Miranda; and this is John, my boy. I wish he wasn't such a bad boy. Make yourself at home, and try to like us and our ways. They ain't very fine; but we mean what we say."

"In what way is John such a bad fellow?" Paul ventured to inquire, by way of setting himself at ease with that young man, who looked at the minister with a certain degree of suspicion, as one of his natural enemies.

Whereupon John's mother made sorrowful confession

of his tricky propensities, of his dislike to church, of his fondness for other boys who were just like him; and Miranda completed the display of John's utter depravity by relating the incident of the cat.

At which the Reverend Paul laughed so heartily that even glum John ventured on a smile, and Miranda had her fun all over again.

When dinner was over, and while the old folks smoked their pipes, Paul persuaded John to show him over the farm; the consequence of which showing was that John returned to Miranda with a puzzled look, and the remark that "that thar minister warn't a bit like any other he ever saw."

"Why, Sis," said the poor fellow, "he laughs just like other people; and made me tell him about every thing on the place. And he likes fishing, and I'm going to show him the creek. And he didn't know what a harrow was till I told him," added John, with a chuckle, "and I'm to show him how to plough."

"So you think he'll do?" queried Miranda, quietly.

"I dunno yet," said John, resuming his cautious look; "I dunno yet—but I think."

Having won over John, Paul's fame soon went through all the country-side; and as he proved himself a tolerable shot, a good fisherman, and a sensible fellow generally, "the boys," who had been so long the plague of Shott-over meeting-house, presently made him their honored captain, without whose presence or countenance no fun could prosper, while they delighted to be for him a guard, sometimes more zealous than wise.

But what avails to recount at length the peaceful triumphs of the Reverend Paul Clifton? His first victory
decided the campaign; and he surprised the brethren at
the next annual Conference meeting by requesting—unless some one else wished the place—to be "continued"
in Shottover another year.

"What Paul Clifton could have found in Shottover?"
was a question which puzzled every body but Paul Clifton himself, till one day—

—Fair, and gentle, and dearly-beloved reader, you
guessed it long ago, didn't you? And I am not such an
ungrateful boor as to disappoint you—

—till one day the bishop was invited to dedicate a new
meeting-house in Shottover; and this done, was requested to "unite in the holy bonds of matrimony"—which
bonds they bear lightly to this day—

THE REVEREND PAUL CLIFTON

AND

MISS MIRANDA LEIGHTON.

John was present, in a great state of mind and shirt-
collar, and after the ceremony was over, and the company had adjourned, privately bestowed his blessing on
Miranda, declaring that "she'd got the best feller that
ever lived for a husband, ef he was a preacher."

ELKANAH BREWSTER'S TEMPTATION.

ELKANAH BREWSTER'S TEMPTATION.

I AM of opinion that the fruit forbidden to our grand-mother Eve was an unripe apple. Eaten, it afflicted Adam with a kind of βελιηχ, in fact, the first colic known to this planet. He, the weaker vessel, sorrowed over his transgression; but I doubt if Eve's repentance was thorough; for the plucking of unripe fruit has been, ever since, a favorite hobby of her sons and daughters, until now our mankind has got itself into such a chronic state of colic, that even Dr. Carlyle declares himself unable to prescribe any Morrison's Pill or other remedial measure to allay the irritation.

Part of this irritation finds vent in a great cry about "legitimate ambition." Somehow, because any American may be President of the United States, almost every American feels himself bound to run for the office. A man thinks small things of himself, and his neighbors think less, if he does not find his heart filled with an in-sane desire, in some way, to attain to fame or notoriety, riches or bankruptcy. Nevertheless, we are not purse-proud, nor, indeed, proud at all, more 's the pity, and re-

ceive a man just as readily whose sands of life have been
doled out to suffering humanity in the shape of patent
pills, as one who has entered Fifth Avenue by the legitimate way of pork and cotton speculations, if only he have
been successful, which I call a very noble trait in the
American character.

Now this is all very well, and, granted that Providence
has placed us here to do what is best pleasing to ourselves, it is surely very noble and grand in us to please
to serve nothing less than our country or our age. But
let us not forget that the English language has such a
little word as duty. A man's talents, and, perhaps, once
in a great while, his wishes, would make him a great man,
if wishes ever did such things, which I doubt, while
duty imperatively demands that he shall remain a little
man. What then?

Elkanah Brewster was going to New York to-morrow.

"What for, boy?" asked old Uncle Shubael, meeting
whom on the fish-wharf, he had bid him a cheery good-
bye.

"To make my fortune," was the bold reply.

"Make yer fortin? You'm a goose, boy! Stick to
yer work here. Fishin' summers an' shoe-makin' winters
—why, there isn't a young feller on the hull Cape makes
as much as you. What's up? Gal gin ye the mitten?
Or what?"

"I don't want to make shoes, nor fish nuther, Uncle
Shub," said Elkanah, soberly, looking the old fellow in
the face—"goin' down to the Banks year arter year in

cold an' fish-gurry, an' peggin' away all winter like mad. I want to be rich, like Captain Crowell; I want to be a gentleman, like that painter-chap that gin me drawin'-lessons, last summer, when I stayed to home."

"Phew! Want to be rich an' a gentleman, eh? Gittin' tu big for yer boots, youngster? What's yer old man du but go down t' the Banks reg'lar every spring? You'm no better 'n he, I guess! Keep yer trade, an' yer trade 'll keep you. A rollin' stun gethers no moss. Dry bread tu home's better 'n roast meat an' gravy abroad."

"All feet don't tread in one shoe, Uncle Shub," said young Brewster, capping the old fellow's proverbs with another. "Don't see why I shouldn't make money 's well's other fellers. It's a free country, an' if a feller wants to try suthin' else 'sides fishin' uv it, what d'yer all want to be down on him fur? I don't want to slave all my days, when other folks ken live in big houses an' ride in 'kerriges, an' all that."

"A'n't ye got bread enough to eat, an' a place to sleep? an' what more's any on 'em got? You stay here; make yer money on the old Cape, where yer father an' grand-'ther made it afore you. Use yer means, an' God 'll give the blessin'. Yer can't honestly git rich anywheres all tu once. Good an' quickly don't often meet. One nail drives out another. Slow an' easy goes fur in a day. Honor an' ease a'n't often bed-fellows. Don't ye be a goose, I tell ye. What's to become o' Hepsy Ann?"

Having delivered himself of which last and hardest shot, Uncle Shubael shouldered his cod-craft, and, with-

F

out awaiting an answer, tugged across the sand-beach for home.

Elkanah Brewster was a Cape-Cod boy, with a pedigree, if he had ever thought of it, as long as any on the Cape, and they are the longest in the land. His forefathers had caught fish to the remotest generation known. The Cape boys take to the water like young ducks; and are born with a hook and line in their fists, so to speak, as the Newfoundland codfish and Bay Chaleur mackerel know to their cost. "Down on old Chatham" there is little question of a boy's calling, if he only comes into the world with the proper number of fingers and toes; he swims as soon as he walks, knows how to drive a bargain as soon as he can talk, goes cook of a coaster at the mature age of nine years, and thinks himself robbed of his birthright if he has not made a voyage to the Banks before his eleventh birthday comes round. There is good stuff in the Cape boys, as the South Street shipowners know, who don't sleep easier than when they have put a Cape man in charge of their best clipper. Quick of apprehension, fertile in resource, shrewd, enterprising, brave, prudent, and, above all, lucky, no better seamen sail the sea.

They are not rich on the Cape, in the Wall Street sense of the word, that is to say. I doubt if Uncle Lew Baker, who was high line out of Dennis last year, and who, by the same token, had to work himself right smartly to achieve that honor—I doubt if this smart and thoroughly wide-awake fellow took home more than three hundred dollars to his wife and children when old

Obed settled the voyage. But then the good wife saves while he earns, and, what with a cow, and a house and garden-spot of his own, and a healthy lot of boys and girls, who, if too young to help, are not suffered to hinder, this man is more forehanded and independent, gives more to the poor about him and to the heathen at the other end of the world, than many a city man who makes and spends his tens of thousands.

Uncle Abijah Brewster, the father of this Elkanah, was an old Banker, which signifies here, not a Wall Street broker-man, but a Grand Bank fisherman. He had brought up a goodly family of boys and girls by his hook-and-line, and, though now a man of some fifty winters, still made his two yearly "fares" to the Banks, in his own trim little pinky, and prided himself on being the smartest and jolliest man aboard. His boys had sailed with him till they got vessels of their own, had learned from his stout heart and strong arm their seamanship, their fisherman's acuteness, their honest daring, and child-like trust in God's providence. These poor fishermen are not rich, as I have said; a dollar looks to them as big as a dinner-plate to some of us, and a moderately flush Wall Street man might buy out half the Cape and not overdraw his bank account. Also they have but little book-learning among them, reading chiefly their Bible, Bowditch, and Nautical Almanac, and leaving theology mostly to the parson on shore, who is paid for it. But they have a conscience, and, knowing a thing to be right, do it bravely, and against all odds. I have seen these men on Sunday, in a fleet of busy "Sun-

day fishers," fish biting all around them, sitting faithfully, ay, and contentedly, with book in hand, sturdily re-
fraining from what the mere human instinct of destruction would strongly impel them to, without counting the
temptation of dollars; and this only because they had
been taught that Sunday was a day of rest and worship,
wherein no man should catch fish, and they knew no
theological quibble or mercantile close-sailing by which
to weather on God's command. It sounds little to us
who have not been tempted, or, if tempted, have gracefully succumbed on the plea that other people do so too;
but how many stock-speculators would see their fellows
buying bargains and making easy fortunes on Sunday
morning, and not forget the ring of Trinity chimes and
go in for dollars? Or which of us denies himself his
Monday morning's paper?

Elkanah had always been what his mother called a
strange boy. He was, indeed, an odd sheep in her flock.
Restless, ambitious, dreamy, from his earliest youth, he
possessed, besides, a natural gift for drawing and sketching, imitating and constructing, that bade fair, unless
properly directed, to make of him that saddest and most
useless of human lumber, a jack-at-all-trades. He profit-
ed more by his limited winter's schooling than his brothers and fellows, and was always respected by the old man
as "a boy that took naterally to book-larnin', and
would be suthin' some day." Of course he went to the
Banks, and acquitted himself there with honor, no man
fishing more zealously or having better luck. But all
the time he was dreaming of his future, counting this

present as nothing, and ready, as soon as Fortune should make him an opening, to cast away this life, and grasp— he had not settled what.

"I dun know what ails him," said his father; "but he don't take kindly to the Banks. Seems to me he kinder despises the work, though he does it well enough. And then he makes the best shoes on the Cape; but he a'n't content, somehow."

And that was just it. He was not contented. He had seen men—"no better than I," thought he, poor fool!—in Boston, living in big houses, wearing fine clothes, putting fair, soft hands into smooth-fitting kid gloves; "and why not I?" he cried to himself continu- ally. Year by year, from his seventeenth to his twenty- first, he was pursued by this demon of "ambition," which so took possession of his heart as to crowd out nearly every thing else, father, mother, work, even pretty Hepzibah Nickerson, almost, who loved him, and whom he also loved truly. They had grown up together, had long loved each other, and had been now two years be- trothed. When Elkanah was "out of his time" and able to buy a share in a vessel, and had made a voyage to the Banks as captain, they were to be married.

The summer before this spring in which our story opens, Elkanah had stayed at home for two months, be- cause of a rheumatism contracted by unusual exposure on the Banks in early spring; and at this time he made the acquaintance of Mr. James Graves, N.A., from New York, spending part of his summer on the Cape in search of the picturesque, which I hope he found. El-

kanah had, as I have said, a natural talent for drawing,
and some of his sketches had that in them which elicited
the approval of Graves, who saw in the young fellow an
untutored genius, or, at least, very considerable promise
of future excellence.   To him there could be but one
choice between shoe-making and "Art;" and finding
that young Brewster made rapid advances under his
desultory tuition, he told him his thoughts: that he
should not waste himself making sea-boots for fishermen,
but enter a studio in Boston or New York, and make
his career as a painter.   It scarcely needed this, however; for Elkanah took such delight in his new proficiency, and got from Graves's stories of artist life such
exalted ideas of the unalloyed felicity of the gentleman
of the brush, that, even had the painter said no word, he
would have worked out that way himself.

"Only wait till next year, when I'm out of my time,"
said he to Graves; and to himself—"This is the opening
for which I have been waiting."

That winter, "my last at shoe-making," he worked
more diligently than ever before, and more good-natured-
ly.   Uncle Abijah was delighted at the change in his
boy, and promised him great things in the way of a lift
next year, to help him to a speedy wedding.   Elkanah
kept his own counsel, read much in certain books which
Graves had left him, and looked impatiently ahead to
the day when, twenty-one years of age, he should be a
free man, able to go whither he listed and do what he
would, with no man authoritatively to say him nay.

And now the day had come; and with I don't know

how few dollars in his pocket, his scant earnings, he had declared to his astounded parents his determination to fish and shoe-make no longer, but to learn to be a painter.

"A great painter,'" that was what he said.

"I don't see no use o' paintin' picters, for. my part," said the old man, despairingly; "can't you larn that, an' fish tu?"

"Famous and rich too," said Elkanah half to himself, looking through the vista of years at the result he hoped for, and congratulating himself in advance upon it; and a proud, hard look settled in his eye, which froze the opposition of father and mother, and was hardly dimmed by encountering the grieved glance of poor Hepsy Ann Nickerson.

Poor Hepsy Ann! They had talked it all over, time and again. At first she was in despair; but when he laid before her all his darling hopes, and painted for her in such glowing colors the final reward which should come to him and her in return for his struggles, when she saw him, her love and pride, before her already transfigured by this rare triumph, clothed with honors, his name in all mouths—dear, loving soul, her heart consented, "ay, if it should break meantime," thought she, as she looked proudly on him through her tears, and said, "Go, in God's name, and God be with you!"

II.

Perhaps we might properly here consider a little whether this young man did well thus to leave father, mother, home, his promised bride, sufficient bread-and-butter, healthy occupation, all, to attempt life in a new direction. Of course, your man who lives by bread alone will "pooh! pooh!" all such folly; and tell the young man to let well enough alone. But consider candidly, and decide: Should Elkanah have gone to New York?

On the whole, I think, yes. For:—

He had a certain talent, and gave fair promise of excellence in his chosen profession.

He liked it, felt strongly impelled toward it. Let us not yet scrutinize too closely the main impelling forces. Few human actions originate solely in what we try to think the most exalted motives.

He would have been discontented for life, had he not had his way. And this should count for something; for much, indeed. Give our boys liberty to try that to which their nature or fancy strongly drives them; to burn their fingers, if that seem best.

Let him go, then; and God be with him! as surely He will be, if the simple, faithful prayers of fair, sad Hepsy Ann are heard. Thus will he, thus only can any, solve that sphinx-riddle of life which is propounded to each passer to-day, as of old in fable-lands; failing to read which, he dies the death of rusting discontent; solving whose mysteries, he has revealed to him the deep secret of his life, and sees and knows what best he may do here for himself and the world.

But what, where, who, is Elkanah Brewster's world?

While we stand reasoning, he has gone. In New York, his friend Graves assisted him to a place in the studio of an artist, whose own works have proved, no less than those of many who have gathered their most precious lessons from him, that he is truly a master of his art. But what are masters, teachers, to a scholar? It's very fine boarding at the Spread-Eagle Hotel; but even after you have fee'd the waiter, you have to chew your own dinner, and are benefited, not by the amount you pay for it, but only by so much of all that with which the boun-teous table is covered as you can thoroughly masticate, easily contain, and healthily digest.

Elkanah began with the soup, so to speak. He brought all his Cape-Cod acuteness of observation to bear on his profession; lived closely, as well he might; studied at-tentively and intelligently; lost no hints, no precious morsels dropping from the master's board; improved slowly, but surely. Day by day he gained in that facili-ty of hand, quickness of observation, accuracy of memory, correctness of judgment, patience of detail, felicity of touch, which, united and perfected and honestly directed, we call genius. He was above no drudgery, shirked no difficulties, and labored at the insignificant sketch in hand to-day as though it were indeed his master-piece, to be hung up beside Raphael's and Titian's; meantime, keeping up poor Hepsy Ann's heart by letters full of a hope bred of his own brave spirit, rather than of any fa-voring circumstances in his life, and gaining his scant bread-and-butter by various honest drudgeries which I will not here recount.

So passed away three years; for the growth of a poor young artist in public favor, and that thing called fame,

F 2

is fearfully slow.   Oftenest he has achieved his best when
the first critic speaks kindly or savagely of him.   What,
indeed, at best, do those blind leaders, but zealously echo
a sentiment already in the public heart, which they vainly endeavor to create (out of nothing) by any awe-in-
spiring formula of big words?

Men grow so slowly!   But then so do oaks; and little
matter, so the growth be straight.

Meantime Elkanah was getting, slowly and by hardest
labor, to have some true conception of his art and his
aims.   He became less and less satisfied with his own
performances; and, having with much pains and anxious
prayers finished his first picture for the Academy, carefully hid it under the bed, and for that year played the
part of independent critic at the Exhibition.   Where-
from resulted some increase of knowledge, though chiefly
negative.

For what positive lesson is taught to any by that yearly show of what we flatter ourselves by calling Art?
Eight hundred and fifteen new paintings this year, shown
by no less than two hundred and eighty-one painters.
When you have gone patiently through and looked at
every picture, see if you don't wish the critics had eyes,
and a little common sense, too.   How many of these two
hundred and eighty-one, if they live to be a hundred,
will ever solve their great riddle? and once solved, how
many would honestly go back to shoe-making?

Why should they not paint?   Because, unless some
of them are poorer men than I think, that is not the
thing they are like to do best; and a man is put into

this world, not to do what he may think or hope will most speedily or effectually place him in the list of this world's illustrious benefactors, but honestly and against all devilish temptations to stick to that thing by which he can best serve and bless—

Whom? A city? A state? A republic? A king?

No, but that person who is nearest to, and most dependent upon him. Look at Charles Lamb—and then at Byron and Shelley.

The growth of a poor young artist into public favor is slow enough. But even poor young artists have their temptations. When Elkanah hung his first picture in the Academy rooms, he thought the world must feel the acquisition. Now the world is a notoriously stupid world, and never does its duty; but kind woman not seldom supplies its omissions. So it happened, that, though the world cared nothing about the picture, Elkanah became at once the centre of admiration to a coterie of young ladies, who thought they were appreciating Art when they flattered an artist, and who, when they read in the papers the gratifying intelligence, invented by some sanguine critic, over a small bottle of Champagne cider, that the American people are rapidly growing in true love for the fine arts, blushingly owned to themselves that their virtuous labors in this direction were not going unrewarded.

Have you never seen them in the Academy, these dear young ladies, who are so constantly foreseeing new Raphaels, Claudes, and Rembrandts? Positively, in this year's Exhibition they are better worth study than the

paintings. There they run, up and down, critical or en-
thusiastical, as the humor strikes: Laura, with big blue
eyes and a loud voice, pitying Isidora because she "has
never met" that dear Mr. Herkimer, who paints such
delicious, dreamy landscapes; and Emily dragging every
body off to see Mr. Smith's great work, ".The Boy and
the Windmill," which, so surprising is his facility, he actually painted in less than twelve days, and which "promises so much for his success and the future of American Art," says this sage young critic, out of whose gray
eyes look.the garnered experiences of almost eighteen
summers.

Whoever desiderates cheap praise, let him cultivate a
beard and a sleepy look, and hang a picture in the Academy rooms. Elkanah received it, you may be sure. It
was thought so romantic, that he, a fisherman — the
young ladies sunk the shoe-maker, I believe—should be
so devoted. to Art. How splendidly it spoke for our
civilization, when even sailors left their vessels, and, ab-
juring codfish, took to canvas and brushes! What admirable courage in him, to come here and endeavor to
work his way up from the very bottom! What praise-
worthy self-denial,—"No! I. is it really so?" cried Miss
Jennie,—when he had left behind him a fair young
bride!

It was as though it had been written, "Blessed is he
who forsaketh father, mother, and wife to paint pictures."

But it is not so written.

It was as if the true aim and glory of every man in a
civilized community should be to paint pictures. Which

has this grain of truth in it, that, in the highest form of human development, I believe every man will be at heart an artist. But then we shall be past picture-painting and exhibitions. Don't you see, that, if the fruit be thoroughly ripe, it needs no violent plucking? or that, if a man is really a painter, he will paint, ay, though he were ten times a shoe-maker, and could never, never hope to hang his pictures on the Academy walls, to win cheap wonder from boarding-school misses, or just regard from judicious critics?

Elkanah Brewster came to New York to make his career, to win nothing less than fame and fortune. When he had struggled through five years of Art-study, and was now just beginning to earn a little money, he began also to think that he had somehow counted his chickens before they were hatched, perhaps, indeed, before the eggs were laid. "Good and quickly come seldom together," said old Uncle Shubael. But then a man who has courage commonly has also endurance; and Elkanah, ardently pursuing from love now what he had first been prompted to by ambition, did not murmur nor despair. For, indeed, I must own that this young fellow had worked up to the highest and truest conception of his art, and felt, that, though the laborer is worthy of his hire, unhappy is the man who lowers his art to the level of a trade. In olden times, the priests did, indeed, eat of the sacrificial meat; but we live under a new and higher dispensation.

III.

MEANTIME, what of Hepsy Ann Nickerson? She had bravely sent her hero out, with her blessing on his aspi- rations. Did she regret her love and trust? I am ashamed to say that these five long, weary years· had passed happily to this young woman. She had her hands full of work at home, where she reigned over a family of brothers and sisters, *vice* her mother, promoted. Hands busied with useful toils, head and heart filled with love and trust of Elkanah, there was no room for unhap- piness. To serve and to be loved: this seems, indeed, to be the bliss of the happiest women I have known— and of the happiest men, too, for that matter. It does not sound logical, and I know of no theory of woman's rights which will satisfactorily account for the phenome- non. But then, there are the facts.

A Cape household is a simpler affair than you will meet with in the city. If any young marrying man waits for a wife who can cook and sew, let him go down to the Cape. Captain Elijah Nickerson, Hepsy Ann's father, was master and owner of the good schooner " Mi- randa," in which excellent but rather strongly-scented ves- sel he generally made yearly two trips to the Newfound- land Banks, to draw thence his regular income ; and it is to be remarked, that his drafts, presented in person, were never dishonored in that foggy region. Uncle Eli- jah—they are all uncles, on the Cape, when they marry and have children, and boys until then—Uncle Elijah, I say, was not uncomfortably off, as things go in those parts. The year before Elkanah went to New York, the old fellow had built himself a brand-new house, and Hepsy Ann was looked up to by her acquaintance as the daughter of a man who was not only brave and honest, but also lucky.

"Elijah Nickerson's new house," as it is still called, and will be, I suppose, until it ceases to be a house, was fitted up inside in a way which put you much in mind of a ship's cabin, and would have delighted the simple heart of good Captain Cuttle. There was no spare space anywhere thrown away, nor any thing suffered to lie loose. Beckets and cleats, fixed into the walls of the sitting-room, held and secured against any possible damage the pipes, fish-lines, dolphin-grains, and sou'westers of the worthy Captain; and here he and his sat, when he was at home, through the long winter evenings, in simple and not often idle content. The kitchen, flanked by the compendious outhouses which make our New England kitchens almost luxurious in the comfort and handiness of every arrangement, was the centre of Hepsy Ann's kingdom, where she reigned supreme, and waged sternest warfare against dirt and disorder. Hence her despotic sway extended over the pantry, an awful and fragrant sanctuary, whither she fled when household troubles, or a letter from Elkanah, demanded her entire seclusion from the outer world, and of whose interior the children got faint glimpses and sniffs only on special and long-remembered occasions; the west room, where her father slept when he was at home, and where the curious searcher might find store of old compasses, worn-out cod-hooks, condemned gurry-knives, and last year's fishing-mittens, all "stowed away against time-o'-need;" the spare room, sacred to the rites of hospitality; the "up-stairs," occupied by the children and Hepsy Ann's self; and finally, but most important of all, the parlor, a mys-terious and hermetically sealed apartment, which almost seemed to me an unconsecrated spot in this little temple of the homely virtues and affections—a room furnished in a style somewhat ostentatious and decidedly uncom-fortable, swept and dusted on Saturday afternoons by Hepsy Ann's own careful hands, sat in by the Captain and her for an hour or two on Sundays in awkward state, then darkened and locked for the rest of the week.

As for the queen and mistress of so much neatness and comfort, I must say, that, like most queens whose likeness I have seen, she was rather plain than strictly beautiful, though, no doubt, her loyal subjects, as in such cases commonly occurs, pictured her to themselves as a very Helen of Troy. If her cheeks had something of the rosy hue of health, cheeks, and arms, too, were well tanned by frequent exposure to the sun. Neither tall nor short, but with a lithe figure, a natural grace and sweet dignity of carriage, the result of sufficient healthy exercise and a pure, untroubled spirit; hands and feet, mouth and nose, not such as a gentleman would particu-larly notice; and straight brown hair, which shaded the only really beautiful part of Hepsy Ann's face, her clear, honest, brave blue eyes: eyes from which spoke a soul at peace with itself and with the outward world, a soul yet full of love and trust, fearing nothing, doubting nothing, believing much good, and inclined to patient endurance of the human weaknesses it met with in daily life, as not perhaps altogether strange to itself. The Cape men are a brave, hardy race; and the Cape women, grave and somewhat silent, not demonstrative in joy or grief, reticent mostly of their anxieties and sorrows, born to endure, in separation from fathers, brothers, lovers, husbands, in dangers not oftener fancied than real, griefs which more fortunate women find it difficult to imagine —these Cape women are worthy mothers of brave men. Of such our Hepsy Ann was a fair example; weaving her somewhat prosaic life into golden dreams in the quiet light of her pantry refuge, happy chiefly because she thought much and carefully for others and had little time for self-brooding; like most genuine heroines, except those of France, living an heroic life without in the least suspecting it.

And did she believe in Elkanah?

Utterly.

And did Elkanah believe in himself?.

Yes—but with certain grave doubts. Here is the difference: the woman's faith is intuition; the man must have a reason for the faith that is in him.

Yet Elkanah was growing. I think a man grows like the walls of a house, by distinct stages: so far the scaffolding reaches, and then a general stoppage while the outer shell is raised, the ladders lengthened, and the work squared off. I don't know, unhappily, the common pro-

cess of growth of the artistic mind, and how far the
light of to-day helps the neophyte to look into the indefinite twilight of. to-morrow; but step by step was
the slow rule of Elkanah's mind, and he had been now
five years an artist, and was held in no despicable repute
by those few who could rightly judge of a man's future
by his past, when first it became very clear to him that
he had yet to find his. specialty in Art—that truth which
he might better represent than any other man.

Don't think five years long to determine so trivial a
point. The right man in the right place is still a rare
phenomenon in the world; and some men spend a life-
time in the consideration of this very point, doubtless
looking to take their chance of real work in the next
world. I mean to say it took Elkanah just five years to
discover, that, though he painted many things fairly, he
did yet put his very soul into none, and that, unless he
could now presently find this, his right place, he had,
perhaps, better stop altogether.

Elkanah considered; but he also worked unceasingly,
feeling that the best way to break through a difficulty is
to pepper away at its outer walls.

IV.

Now while he was firing away wearily at this fortress,
which held, he thought, the deepest secret of his life,
Hepsy Ann sat in her pantry, her serene soul troubled
with unwonted fears. Captain Elijah Nickerson had sailed out in his stanch schooner in earliest spring, for the

Banks. The old man had been all winter meditating a surprise; and his crew were in unusual excitement, peering out at the weather, consulting almanacs, prophesying to outsiders a late season, and winking to each other a cheerful disbelief of their own auguries. The fact is, they were intending to slip off before the rest, and perhaps have half their fare of fish caught before the fleet got along.

No plan could have succeeded better, up to a certain point. Captain Elijah got off to sea full twelve days earlier than any body else, and was bowling merrily down toward the eternal fog-banks when his neighbors were yet scarce thinking of gathering up their mittens and sea-boots. By the time the last-comers arrived on the fishing-ground, one who had spoken the "Miranda" some days before, anchored and fishing away, reported that they had, indeed, nearly wet her salt, by which is meant that she was nearly filled with good, sound codfish. The men were singing as they dressed their fish, and Captain Elijah, sitting high up on the schooner's quarter, took his pipe out of his mouth, and asked, as the vessel rose on the sea, if they had any news to send home, for three days more like that would fill him up.

That was the last word of Captain Elijah Nickerson's ever heard by men now living.

Whether the "Miranda" was sunk by an iceberg; whether run down in the dark and silent watches of the night by some monster packet or swift hurling steamer, little recking the pale fisher's light feebly glimmering up from the surface of the deep; or whether they went

down at their anchors, in the great gale which set in on
the third night, as many brave men have done before,
looking their fate steadfastly in the face for long hours,
and taking time to bid each other farewell ere the great
sea swallowed them: the particulars of their hapless
fate no man may know, till the dread day when the sea
shall give up its dead.

Vainly poor Hepsy Ann waited for the well-known
signal in the offing, daily walking to the shore, where
kind old Uncle Shubael, now long superannuated, and
idly busying himself about the fish-house, strove to cheer
her fainting soul by store of well-chosen proverbs, and
yarns of how, aforetimes, schooners not larger and not so
stout as the "Miranda," starting early for the Banks, had
been blown southward to the West Indies, and, when the
second-fare men came in with their fish, had made their
appearance laden with rich cargoes of tropical molasses
and bananas. Poor Hepsy Ann! what need to describe
the long-drawn agony which grew with the summer
flowers, but did not wane with the summer sun? Hour
after hour, day after day, she sat by her pantry-window,
looking with wistful eyes out over the sand, to that spot
where the ill-fated "Miranda" had last been seen, but
never should appear again—another

> "poor lone Hannah,
> Sitting by the window, binding shoes"—

cheeks paling, eyes dimming, with that hope deferred
which maketh the heart sick. Pray God you never may
be so tried, fair reader! If, in these days, she had not
had the children to keep and comfort, she has since

told me, she could scarce have borne it. To calm their fears, to soothe their little sorrows, to look anxiously, more anxiously than ever before, after each one of her precious little brood, became now her chief solace.

Thus the long weary days rolled away, each setting sun crushing another hope, until at last the autumn storms approached, the last Banker was safe home; and by this time it was plain, even to poor Hepsy Ann's faithful heart, that her dead would not come back to her.

"If only Elkanah were here!" she had sometimes sighed to herself; but in all these days she wrote him no word. And he, guessing nothing of her long, silent agony, himself sufficiently bemired in his slough of despond, working away with sad, unsatisfied heart in his little studio, hoping yet for light to come to his night, was, in truth, so full of himself, that Hepsy Ann had little of his thoughts. Shall I go further, and admit that sometimes this poor fellow dimly regretted his pledged heart, and faintly murmured, "If only I were free, then I might do something"?

If only the ship were rid of her helmsman, then indeed would she go—somewhere.

At last—it was already near Thanksgiving—the news reached Elkanah. "I thought you'd ha' been down afore this to see Hepsy Ann Nickerson in her trouble," said an old coasting-skipper to him, with mild reproach, handing him a letter from his mother—of all persons in the world! Whereupon, seeing ignorance in Elkanah's inquiring glance, he told the story.

Elkanah was as one in a maze. Going to his little room, he opened his mother's letter, half dreading to find here a detailed repetition of what his heart had just taken in. But the letter was short.

"My Son Elkanah:—Do you not know that Captain Elijah Nickerson will never come home from the Banks, and that Hepsy Ann is left alone in the world?

"'For this cause shall a man leave his father and mother, and be joined to his wife, and they two shall be one flesh.'"

That was all.

Elkanah sat on his stool, before his easel, looking vacantly at the unfinished picture, as one stunned and breathless. For the purport of this message was not to be mistaken. Nor did his conscience leave him in doubt as to his duty. O God! was this, indeed, the end? Had he toiled, and hoped, and prayed, and lived the life of an anchorite these five years only for this? Was such faith, such devotion, so rewarded?

But had any one the right to demand this sacrifice of him? Was it not a devilish temptation to take him from his calling, from that work in which God had evidently intended him to work for the world? Had he a right to spoil his life, to belittle his soul, for any consideration? If Hepsy Ann Nickerson had claims, had not he also, and his Art? If he were willing, in this dire extremity, to sacrifice his love, his prospects of married bliss, might he not justly require the same of her? Was

not Art his mistress? Thus whispered the insidious
devil of Selfishness to this poor, tempted, anguished soul.
" Yea," whispered another still, small voice; " but is
not Hepsy Ann your promised wife?" And those fatal
words sounded in his heart: " For this cause shall a
man leave his father and mother, and be joined to his
wife."

"Lord, inspire me to do what is right!" prayed poor
mazed Elkanah, sinking on his knees at his cot-side.

But presently, through his blinding tears, " Lord, give
me strength to do the right!"

V.

And then, when he awoke next morning, the world
seemed another world to him. The foundations of his
life were broken loose. Tears were no longer, nor
prayers. But he went about slowly, and with loving
hands, packing up his brushes, pallets, paints, easel—all
the few familiar objects of a life which was his no longer,
and on which he seemed to himself already looking as
across some vast gulf of years. At last all was done.
A last look about the dismantled garret, so long his
workshop, his home, where he had grown out of one life
into another, and a better, as he thought—out of a narrow circle into a broader. And then, away for the Cape.
No farewells, no explanations to friends, nothing that
should hold out to his sad soul any faintest hope of a
return to this garret, this toil, which now seemed to him
more heaven than ever before.

Thus this Adam left his paradise, clinging to his Eve.

It was the day before Thanksgiving when Elkanah arrived at home. Will any one blame him, if he felt little thankful? if the thought of the Thanksgiving turkey was like to choke him, and the very idea of giving thanks seemed to him a bitter satire? Poor fellow! he forgot that there were other hearts to whom Thanksgiving turkey was little tempting.

The Cape folk are not demonstrative. They have warm hearts, but the old Puritan ice has never quite melted away from the outer shell.

"Well, Elkanah, glad to see you, boy!" said his father, looking up from his corner by the stove; "how's things in New York?" Father and son had not met for three years. But, going into the kitchen, he received a warm grasp of the hand, and his mother said, in her low, sweet voice, "I knew you'd come." That was all. But it was enough.

How to take his sad face over to Elijah Nickerson's new house? But that must be done, too. Looking through the little sitting-room window, as he passed, he saw pale-faced Hepsy Ann sitting quietly by the table, sewing. The children had gone to bed. He did not knock; why should he?· but, walking in, stood silent on the floor. A glad, surprised smile lit up the sad, wan face, as she recognized him, and, stepping to his side, said, "Oh, Elkanah! I knew you'd come. How good of you!" Then, abashed to have so committed herself and him, she shrank to her chair again.

Let us not intrude further on these two. Surely Elka-

nah Brewster had been less than man, had he not found
his hard heart to soften, and his cold love to warm, as
he drew from her the story of her long agony, and saw
this weary heart ready to rest upon him, longing to be
comforted in his strong arms.

The next day a small sign was put up at Abijah
Brewster's door—

BOOTS AND SHOES

MADE AND MENDED

BY

ELKANAH BREWSTER.

It was arranged that he should work at his trade all
winter. In the spring he was to have his father's vessel, and the wedding would be before he started for the
Banks.

So the old life was put on again. I will not say that
Elkanah was thoroughly content—that there were no bitter longings, no dim regrets, no faint questionings of
Providence. But hard work is a good salve for a sore
heart; and in his honest toils, in his care for Hepsy Ann
and her little brood, in her kind heart, which acknowl-
edged with such humility of love all he did for her and
all he had cast away for her, he found his reward.

The wedding was over, a quiet affair enough, and Elkanah was anchored on the Banks, with a brave, skillful
crew, and plenty of fish. His old luck had not deserted him; wherever he dropped anchor, there the cod
seemed to gather; and, in the excitement of catching
fish and guarding against the dangers of the Banks, the

G

New York life seemed presently forgotten; and, once more, Elkanah's face wore the old, hopeful calm which belonged there. Art, who had been so long his tyrant mistress, was at last cast off.

Was she?

As he sat, one evening, high on the quarter, smoking his pipe, in that calm, contemplative mood which is the smoker's reward for a day of toil—the little vessel pitching bows under in the long, tremendous swell of the Atlantic, the low drifting fog lurid in the light of the setting sun, but bright stars twinkling out, one by one, overhead, in a sky of Italian clearness and softness, it all came to him, that which he had so long, so vainly sought, toiled for, prayed for in New York—his destiny.

Why should he paint heads, figures, landscapes, objects with which his heart had never been really filled?

But now, as in one flash of divinest intelligence, it was revealed to him! This sea, this fog, this sky, these stars, this old, old life, which he had been almost born into, O, blind bat indeed, not to have seen, long, long ago, that this was your birthright in Art! not to have felt, in your innermost heart, that this was indeed that thing, if any thing, which God had called you to paint!

For, this Elkanah had drunk in from his earliest youth, this he understood to its very core; but the poor secret of that other life, which is so draped about with the artistic mannerisms and fashionable Art of New York, or any other civilized life, he had never rightly appreciated.

In that sunset-hour was born a painter!

VI.

It chanced, that, a few months ago, I paid my accustomed summer visit to an old friend, living near Boston— a retired merchant he calls himself. He began life as a cabin-boy, became, in time, master of an Indiaman, then, partner in a China house, and after many years' residence in Canton, returned some years ago, heart and liver whole, to spend his remaining days among olden scenes. A man of truest culture, generous heart, and rarely erring taste. I never go there without finding something new and admirable.

"What am I to see this time?" I asked, after dinner, looking about the drawing-room.

"Come. I'll show you."

He led me up to a painting, a sea-piece: a schooner, riding at her anchor, at sunset, far out at sea, no land in sight, sails down, all but a little patch of storm-sail fluttering wildly in the gale, and heavily pitching in a great, grand, rolling sea; around, but not closely enveloping her, a driving fog-bank, lurid in the yellow sheen of the setting sun; above her, a few stars dimly twinkling through a clear blue sky; on the quarter-deck, men sitting, wrapped in all the paraphernalia of storm-clothing, smoking and watching the roll of the sea.

"What do you think?" asked Captain Eastwick, interrupting my rapt contemplation.

"I never in my life saw so fine a sea-view. Whose can it be?"

" A Cape-Cod fisherman's."

" But he is a genius!" cried I, enthusiastically.

" A great, a splendid genius!" said my friend, quietly.

" And a fisherman?"

" Yes, and shoe-maker."

" What a magnificent career he might make! Why don't you help him? What a pity to bury such a man in fish-boots and cod-livers!"

" My dear," said Captain Eastwick, "you are a goose. The highest genius lives above the littleness of making a career. This man needs no Academy prizes or praises. To my mind, his is the noblest, happiest life of all."

Whereupon he told me the story which I have endeavored to relate.

ONE PAIR OF BLUE EYES.

ONE PAIR OF BLUE EYES.

WHOEVER cares to get at the remainder of this in-
ventory of charms, the property of one Lizzy Albertson, but now sometime in the care and guardianship
of George Markham, Artist, must read this story through
to the end.   I have not yet determined at what point
therein Miss Lizzie shall come upon the stage.

"The serenity of fortunate people," says La Roche-
foucauld, "comes from the calm which good fortune
gives to their temper."   To show what serenity of-mind
and contentment of heart may come to one whom fortune
has treated with persistent unkindness is in part the object of this true story.

Six years ago my school friend, George Markham, returned to our little New England city, his birthplace
and early home, after an absence of many years in Italy,
devoted to the study of his profession, Painting.

He left us a thoughtful, quiet boy of nineteen.   He returned, a man of twenty-seven, bearded, mustacheoed,
sunburned, grave, but gentle still.

George was left an orphan at the age of seven; and

was at that time adopted by the family of a maternal uncle, a worthy and large-hearted ship-carpenter, who, though he had a growing family of his own to provide for, could not see the poor little boy thrown helpless upon the tender mercies of strangers. This uncle, by name Williams, gave to George such an education as was within his limited means; gave him shelter, food and clothing; and seeing the boy's decided aversion to the avuncular trade of ship-building, and his just as decided bent for drawing and sketching, was kind enough not to oppose him too strongly, but permitted him to devote his scant pocket-money and spare hours to a resident master of design, who carried his pupil quickly through the elements of outline, shading, and perspective, and there left him to shift for himself, that being, in fact, as far as he could carry him.

At fourteen George entered a "store" as clerk. On his nineteenth birthday he set out for Italy, with bright hopes, a scanty wardrobe, a few Italian and English books, and the immense sum of two hundred and fifty dollars, the savings of his young life-time, whereupon to live out the weary days of his novitiate in Art.

You see, in a smart little town such as ours was at that time, the good folks know a great deal about each other's business and private affairs; and so George's "circumstances" and struggles and hopes were public property, and, you may depend, were freely enough discussed at the diurnal gatherings of grannies male and female. There was the usual talk of your shrewd man of the world, who knows all about the future, having examined

it thoroughly through his own private millstone; the
usual talk about the folly of young men above following
the professions of their fathers, from wood-sawing up, as
though Caste were a Divine Institution; the usual small
sneer at youthful aspirations: this from a man, you may
be sure! women do not sneer at any thing which tends
upward—as though one should not think of climbing
till his limbs are stiff with age and rust. Little good
was prophesied of the boy who might have become a
ship-carpenter, or a "store-keeper," or perhaps, had he
gone a whaling—ours is a whaling port—might eventual-
ly, barring accidents, have attained even the dignity of
whaling-skipper, but who perversely chose to throw away
his opportunities, and waste his youth and time in foreign
parts, "learning to do what would never be of use to any
one."

Of course we boys, his school-mates, were with George.
Not that we had elevated notions about Art; indeed, so
far as I remember, what ideas we had at all upon the
subject were of the crudest. But boys like to see boys
have their way; and though George said very little of
his hopes, his hopeful face told a tale which was not
greek to any of us. If our school-mate heard any of the
sneers and ill auguries which passed around, they did not
affect him; his sky was without a cloud as yet. Moreover, truth to say, the good townsfolk really liked George,
and though naturally thinking him sadly mistaken,
pretty unanimously wished him well. The boy had been
learning all his life that bitterly wholesome lesson, earliest
taught the children of misfortune, to suit himself readily
G 2

to the humors and prejudices of those who affected more or less his limited happiness, and to take his point, if it were worth taking, with a respectful " by-your-leave " to those who differed from him. Not so obstinately as imploringly persistent, George enlisted his townsmen's sympathies; and as they knew he was wrong, they could and did afford him their best wishes, to cheer him on his lonely way.

Arrived in Rome, he went earnestly to work. His letters spoke little, even of his hopes; but they were never gloomy. Besides amusing descriptions of the strange sights and people he met, scraps of which from time to time gained admission to the columns of our weekly paper, to honest Mrs. Williams's great delight, and enthusiastic words on the wonders of Art with which he was delighting and instructing himself, there was very little. Nothing, in fact, except, in his letters to Mr. Williams, always an assurance that he was conscientiously using his opportunities, and that he hoped by and by to accomplish something: which last was so modestly vague that I think it gained him little credit with any one but Mrs. Williams, who in her secret heart firmly believed him a budding Michael Angelo.

How he lived through those days, this young Art student, I have never discovered. Two hundred and fifty dollars could not hold out forever, even in the Eternal City, and what came after I can not imagine, never, thank fortune! having been in Rome, or an Art student, myself. Doubtless there was earnest and honest and modest endeavor, cheered by the sometimes faint but never silent

voice within, which assures the man that he has found
his vocation in life. I fancy Providence somehow
watches over these young ones, who, full of faith, and in-
cipient good works let us say, so ingenuously thrust
themselves into places where there would seem to be no
openings of the better sort for young men. I suspect
that George was oftentimes inconveniently near starving,
and had long need of a new coat before he got it. But
these are by-gones: fears whose season is past; clouds
whose storms only aided to ripen the hopes of those days
into the fair fruition of these.

George did not starve; and he did become so far pro-
ficient in his Art as by and by to attract the attention
of the picture buyers. Presently some liberal-hearted
Americans gave him orders which enabled him to work
more at ease. Great again was honest Mrs. Williams's
joy, when so much of young Markham's success was
heralded to the town in our newly-established Daily, that
big-typed messenger of stale news.

Seven years had passed when George returned to us,
having achieved during his long absence, as in part before mentioned, much hair, some reputation, and a very
pretty little account at the " Whalemen's Security Bank;"
part of which last he devoted, as was right, to cancelling
the pecuniary part of his boyhood's debt to good Uncle
Williams, while the remainder was quite sufficient to warrant him in lying on his oars for a summer, enjoying a
holiday he had fairly earned.

Now our town is a place famous for summer amuse-
ments: bathing, boating, fishing, idling, flirting, picnick-

ing, what not. There are plenty of ways and means to
kill time and spend money, as sundry merchants of
your great Gotham know to their cost, whose wives
and daughters rustle and rusticate amongst us annually,
pending the expiration of Mr. Merriam's heated term.
George, of course, spent the summer with us. During
his absence the little town had grown, after the manner
of American towns, to be nearly a city; many of its
worthy citizens had become wealthy and fashionable.

To their credit be it said, that George, who had by no
means been forgotten, was one of the fashions of the
season. His studio, where he had unrolled a few of his
paintings, and set up his modest collection of souvenirs
of travel, was quite a place of pilgrimage; and fairer
pilgrims, or more admiring, sure no lucky young bache-
lor hermit could ask. Invitations to boating and fishing
parties, to picnics, to tea (we do not give dinners), were
showered upon him; and wherever he showed his quiet,
jolly old mug he was hailed by friends. My friend was
not a hero, only a simple good-hearted young fellow;
but he would have been a brute had he not seen and
enjoyed the liking of his townsmen.

Being now, as I have said, in his twenty-seventh year,
and having the proper and natural longing for domestic
happiness, a hearth of his own, *et cetera*, it seemed to
me that this was the time for George, as a reasonable
man, to choose him a wife. Moreover, being an artist,
no very lucrative profession at best, and having his own
bread to earn and way to make, I, who am a lawyer (I
have handed my business card to the editor of this jour-

nal, and will be most happy to attend to any business in my line, with promptness and dispatch), I, who am, I trust, a sensible man, thought it clearly his duty, other things being equal, to marry some young woman with a portion of her own.

N. B.—It may be as well here to inform the reader that I am not a mercenary wretch, but only a right-minded and tolerably clear-headed man ; that I do not, though a lawyer, " advocate the sacrifice of the holiest affections upon the altar of Mammon," and so on ; but on the contrary believe that no marriage without love can prosper ; just as firmly as I believe that no marriage without a sufficiency of bread and butter, and its adjuncts, can be at all comfortable. Of both these great hymeneal facts a married lawyer of thirty years may be supposed a capable judge. There remained in this case, therefore, only one of two courses : to marry wealth, as I proposed ; or to wait 'till he got rich. But I think it would take a poor devil artist some years to amass the funds needed to buy precisely the article in the matrimonial market which would best suit him.

With these views of life, and my love for George, I did not behold without a certain degree of dismay the establishment of an atrocious flirtation between my friend and a young woman of my acquaintance, the Lizzy Albertson before named ; who therefore comes now upon the stage. Lizzy, a great pet of my wife's and much at our house, was a charming girl, bright, graceful, fair-haired, and blue-eyed ; an orphan, and penniless ; being dependent upon an uncle who could be-

stow upon her nothing more substantial than a father-
ly affection, her education, and a home. A sweet little
girl, who had so many faults that no one of her friends
who petted her but also gave her good advice; and yet
so perfect that no man but a fool would have risked his
soul by tinkering at her, or in any way trying to amend
her. One can not help feeling a great pity for this one,
at least, of the many products of our republican school
system, which so democratically jumbles together poor
and rich, but while thus establishing a common bond between the social extremes, is, I fear, more apt to affect
the poor girl with aristocratic tastes than to infuse republican simplicity into the hearts and minds of the
wealthier. Looking at Lizzy, one was tempted to echo
Mr. Harold Skimpole's buoyant wish that "there might
be no brambles of sordid realities in such a path as that.
It should be strewn with roses; it should be through
bowers where there was no spring, autumn, nor winter,
but perpetual summer. Age or change should never
wither it. The base word money should never be
breathed near it."

If George had been a rich man, here, I think, had
been a wife just suited to him. But not for a poor fellow! and this I determined to tell him.

It is but fair to say that on communicating my views
to my wife, that exemplary matron declined utterly to
look at the matter with me; declaring bluntly that people ought to trust a little, in such cases, to Providence,
the world ("which is good enough in the main," said
this unsophisticated woman), and to themselves; at-

tempting, moreover, to clinch her sophistries by asking if I, the reader's humble servant, "thought of such things when courting her?" To which I instantly replied that I was a lawyer and not an artist; that she was her dear self and not Lizzy Albertson; and that plainly there was no parallel between the cases; which propositions I proceeded to demonstrate on the spot by a kiss on as rosy a pair of lips as you will meet in a sunny day's travel in our part of the country; and having thus effectually closed her mouth, I beat a victorious retreat, and sped upon my mission. Oh these women! They can never look at such a merely common-sense matter sensibly! If they but sniff a wedding in the far distance, see how they prick back their ears and rush to lend their mighty help.

"My dear young friend," said I, entering the studio, where George sat in blissful contemplation of his cigar-smoke, "I understand you are making up to that Lizzy Albertson." I opened the case in this wise in order, if possible, to take the witness by surprise.

"Well?" said George, very little ruffled, I must confess.

"It is not well; she's poor," said I, righteously scorning all subterfuge, and coming at once to the point.

"Well?"

"She's a dear, frail, unsophisticated creature, who will make some wealthy man a happy wife, if he has a heart big enough for her. She is bright and cheery and thoroughly good; but she has not strength enough to struggle with poverty and adversity. You will only tie your hands. You ought to do better."

"Bosh!"

Now came my last and best shot.

"And so ought Lizzy.. Such as she are meant to enjoy, not to help accumulate. With a husband who can
afford to cherish and indulge her, she will live her natural life out. With you, poor fellow, why it's positively
selfish in you to ask her to be your wife."

George was not much of a mathematician, but he had
studied Euclid enough to know that a straight line is
the shortest distance between two points.

"That looks fair," said he, in reply to my last. "I'll
go over and ask her about it."

Will you believe it? The fellow actually went over
to my house, stated the case honorably to Miss Lizzy,
and, of course, was accepted!

That was the end of my match-marring. They were
married at the beginning of winter and immediately removed to New York, that centre of art and money. Up
to their wedding-day, I ceased not to warn both parties
to this rash wooing; to lecture them on economy and
self-denial; to alarm them by eloquent pictures of the
missions of poverty. But what availed my croaking
when their hearts were filled with love-illumined pictures of the future? sketches drawn by Cupid's own master hand? To such young people as these life seems to
promise every thing, and the problem of happiness and
fortune is solved before it is read. What dreams they
dreamed! Of a neat cottage home of their own, where
the taste and industry of the wife should make up for
all monetary deficiencies in the husband; of a quiet and

obscure life wherein these two love-stricken souls should be a happy all in all to each other; of the great master-piece, already sketched in thought, by which George should achieve fame and wealth, as it were at one stroke of the brush; of a consequent tour through Europe: revisiting with her he loved best the long familiar scenes and life of Italy; a well-earned competence to settle down to, in old age, among congenial spirits. What avails the rehearsal? Have we not all alike dreamed such dreams, and seen such visions?

So they removed to New York, where George set up his studio, and divided his hours of leisure between his wife and the master-piece, which last had got little fur-ther yet than the mind of the painter. For to produce this master-piece needs not only will, but thought, expe-rience, study; for these, indeed, are they not the com-ponent parts of all true Genius? Here George worked out happier days than in that bitter struggle of his youth he had ever hoped to see. The man who has a vocation he loves, and can afford to work at it; who has a wife he loves, and a home which she makes cheerful; who has youth, health, a good name, and a rising reputation in his profession: surely this man need ask no more of the gods? No more? Yes; let him seek to want more. Let him pray God to save his soul from the stagnation of utter content; from the fatal taint of a too easy success. There is in every human heart a latent genius for martyr-dom; and only when this finer, nobler instinct of self-sac-rifice is brought into active life does the wearied soul grow upward.

Life in a great city is more systematized, better regulated, greatly more endurable, than in the country. But city life is fatally one-sided. In these close streets, and between these high walls, the poor human flower receives the light but slantingly; and grows sadly awry. Think! the body is so very unimportant a portion of the being! But in your great city all is prepared for its comfort. Your paved streets, "gas and hot water," your stuffed arm-chairs, cosy libraries, lined with well-bound books you do not read, multitudinous servants, and general non-necessity for exertion: these are what most effectually embrute the average man; pampering the body till its pauper clamors drown out the feeble cry of the soul. For, counting in the schools, the libraries, the charities, all the grand benefits of a great American city, what are after all the influences which most irresistibly and universally affect all life there? Firkin and Flora McFlimsy, Wall Street and Fifth Avenue— are not these your gods, O Gotham? The merchant who in the general haste to be rich prefers, like a good whist-player, to take his game by tricks, rather than by honors; the belle whom an overwhelming prosperity binds down in fatal fetters to dress and the next party; these are really they who teach the young city idea how to shoot the shafts of life. Let us rejoice if young men and women distrust the city, and seek for a freer atmosphere in the country.

That is to say, the theory of so-called respectable American city life is that every man of family has an income of at least five thousand a year; the practice is to "board" and sponge on the hospitalities of your friends for society, until you move into your brown stone front. Wherefore Mr. and Mrs. George Markham, having "moved" into New York, had my hearty approval when they moved out of it, and into a modest country cottage where, as he remarked, he and his Lizzy could "make as much noise as they pleased"—which was, to be sure, an important consideration. Here the young wife, thrown upon her own resources for house management, came out in a triumphant way which proves to me that it is no easy matter for stupid teachers and a more stupid system of society to spoil a genuine woman. We complain of inefficient wives and mothers, but what do we not do to spoil our daughters for all future usefulness? Is it too much to say that no average mind can come out unimpaired from the usual course of platitudes, called lessons, in boarding-schools? The school system of this country is in theory the grandest, most liberal in the world; in effect the most narrowing, superficial, abominable. Boys recover in some measure, in their forced battle with the world, from the dullness and intellectual impotence gathered in the schools. The girl, poor soul, jumps from the finishing school into society, makes haste to forget what she never was made to understand, and acquires instead what—God help her —we abuse her for knowing after awhile.

And yet, and yet, where can you find one of these much abused ones, that, given proper opportunity and the inspiration of a worthy man's love, does not justify all that the most ardent admirers of woman's powers

can ask of her? Let us not be too hard on Flora Mc-
Flimsy. The seeds of noble deeds, of patient endurance
and loving sacrifice, of all gentleness and goodness, are
not extinct but only slumbering in

> "That rather decayed but well-known work of Art,
> Which Miss Flora persisted in calling her heart."

Perhaps some day, in some decennial panic, she too may
be fortunately ruined; and thus relieved, let us believe
that Flora will make a good sensible wife, as (I believe)
every woman would, could she have a good sensible
husband.

But to return to our sheep, our lovers that is to say.
George and his Lizzy were established in their country
cottage, which my wife, having paid it a visit of inspec-
tion, pronounced a kind of terrestrial paradise, without
serpent or forbidden fruit. As for the famous skeleton
in the closet, this was before the era of hoops, and, to the
best of my recollection, my wife made mention of no
such anatomical preparation.

In the winter of 1855, Mr. and Mrs. Williams, George's
uncle and aunt, sailed for the West Indies, on a health
trip. The children, four in number, the eldest two had
died years before, were placed at various schools until
their parents' return; all except Ruth, the youngest, who
came to George. The vessel in which the parents sailed
has never been heard from. Weeks and months elapsed
without news from the absent, and at last, late in spring,
when it was but too certain that in the bitter storms of
that winter the ill-fated bark had gone down, it became
necessary to do something for the future of the orphaned

children. Mr. Williams was thought well to do; but when all was settled there was found to be nothing left. What was to become of them?

Of course it was a great and unexpected misfortune; and every body felt excessively sorry for the poor things whose future was thus so strangely overcast with woe, if not with want. But then, sympathy don't fill the stomachs or clothe the backs of orphans, more's the pity, and with all our sorrow these might have been put on the street, had not George at once made up his mind to care for them as for his own flesh and blood; rightly conceiving this a proper return for the obligations conferred upon his own childhood.

But how? The scant income of a young artist makes but a sparing pot of his own to boil. Whence will come the means to pay butcher's and baker's, tailor's, shoe-maker's and teacher's bills, adequate to the furnishing of these four young stomachs, backs, and brains? Has any one who reads this experienced the almost hopeless and helpless despair of a conscientious man who sees suddenly looming up before him some great duty, seemingly impossible of fulfillment? a rock not to be avoided, but on which the poor mariner thinks surely to make shipwreck? Only one who has known this bitter experience can appreciate the state of mind in which my poor friend found himself while thus divided between duty and—duty.

One one side Conscience: You owe every thing to the parents of these children—dare you see them suffer?

To which Expediency: But you have your wife, and,

in the early future, your child. There lies your first duty. And have you not paid abundantly, in hard-earned money, this debt of yours?

Conscience: Was your debt to be paid with money?

Expediency: But your wife, your future? Can you discharge this duty, if duty it be?

Conscience—troublesome as ever, and determined (she is a woman) to have the last word: A man can always do his duty.

"I sat and tore my hair and puzzled my brain about the matter, reproached myself for having married, begrudged myself the short happiness of my married life, thought you, my prudent friend, a very Solomon of wisdom, and myself a donkey, that I had not seen as you did—when suddenly two white arms encircled my neck, and the dearest eyes in the world looked hope into mine.

"'I think, my dear, you had better go on to-morrow, and bring back the children. All will be ready for them when you get them here. Now drive away the clouds from your face. I know you have been wishing me back into my girlhood, and all sorts of horrid things—and I should deserve it all if I stood for a moment between you and honest duty. Let us work together, my dear husband, and courage! Don't forget that there is a Providence. Did I not promise to be a helper to you?' And with such words of holiest comfort to my heart, my dear one ran off to get dinner on the table. That settled the matter," said George, repeating his wife's words with tears in his honest eyes.

The children came to George. The little cottage,

which seemed before hardly big enough to contain themselves, suddenly proved equal to the accommodation of
all the new-comers. They did not starve, as George
had half imagined they would; indeed that witch of all
witches, Mrs. George, by some potent sorcery made her
allowance hold out nearly as well as before. "And really
you have no idea, Mr. Smith," said she to me not long
after, "how much they help me about the house. Active little bodies, they do a hundred things for me, and
gladly, which would cost me worlds of trouble otherwise.
I love them as though they were our own; and they
fill the house and indeed the whole garden with the
cheerful music of their childish prattle and laughter.
I'm sure I could not do without them; and then," winking demurely at her husband, "I tell George we've got
them at a great bargain, for they have all had the measles
and whooping-cough."

Having now really begun to do this plain but hard
duty, if I were merely inventing a pretty story, I think
I should at this stage of the proceedings let some rich
curmudgeon of an uncle die, full of years and dollars,
and will a fortune to the most deserving of heroes and
heroines. But the providence of story-tellers differs
somewhat from the Providence of God. Man is glad to
take the will for the deed; but God accepts the honest
sacrifice, and divinely turns it to the giver's greatest good.
There has intervened in the present case, I am sorry to
say, no rich uncle, or other pecuniary convenience. I
have to report that it has required no little contriving
on the part of Mrs. George, and no slight labor on that of

her husband, to duly join together the financial ends. I am not sure but George had a new coat oftener in his early days in Italy even than he has now; and my wife tells me in strictest confidence that poor Mrs. George has not had a new silk dress in nearly three years! It took the entire savings of two long years to purchase what the little woman liked better, a piano, which looks rather out of place, though, in their little cottage, until you hear Lizzy playing. In fact, though they have managed to keep body and soul together, and are somehow a confoundedly jolly family, my wife and I agree that they have had monstrous difficulties to contend with, and find no rule to account for their happiness. They do not seem to mind, though. I do not know a more blithe or cheerful little woman than Lizzy, who not being able to afford a doctor, goes singing up and down the house all day, in very vulgar good health, with cheeks the color of the reddest peony in her garden. As for George, high art was too high for him, and he has taken to painting portraits, which he does so well, and with so pleasing a grace, as though the highest aspiration of his soul were satisfied in taking off the pimply nose of Mr. Alderman Bloggs, that if the days should happen to grow to twice their length this coming summer, I am sure all his hours would be filled with sitters.

And the master-piece? Well, the master-piece is laid over. Many a good man and true, in this world, can not spare time from his bread-and-butter work for his master-piece. And the world jogs on all the same; as though master-pieces were of little importance, which I sometimes think is very nearly the case.

And Italy? Kind reader, I am sorry; I do not think little Lizzy will ever see Italy, nor George ever show her the scenes of his early fears, hopes, and triumphs. They have their hopes and their plans; but there are disappointments in all lives; and that man is to be pitied who thinks to do a real duty without sacrificing something. Lizzy will scarcely see Italy; but Harry Williams goes to college next year, fully prepared, and Jeannette, his eldest sister, is head of her class in the best girl's school in the country. Tommy and Ruth will take their turns in time, and to them will probably succeed a couple of youngsters whose laughing brown eyes Lizzy would not give for a dozen Italies.

When I read in my morning paper of the gay parties and fine winter doings in Washington and elsewhere, where the American citizen drinks deep at the fountain of social pleasure; when my friends boast of American beauty or grace abroad; when I think of the many joys society and the great world hold out to one who has not only a beautiful face but a good heart and a bright spirit—reading of these things, I sometimes think longingly of our little Blue Eyes, with her eager enjoyment of life, her fine brave spirits and keen appreciation of all innocent pleasures, and all beautiful things. These might have been hers, too, I say to myself. She would have shone among the fairest and brightest. None would have more enjoyed, none would have better graced such scenes as these.

But, on the whole—do you pity her?

H

.

.

MEHETABEL ROGERS'S CRANBERRY SWAMP.

MEHETABEL ROGERS'S CRANBERRY SWAMP.

I.

" MAN proposes, God disposes;" so says an old proverb. Sometimes women propose.

Mehetabel Rogers proposed to go to Boston to-morrow. She had been there once before in her life, for
Boston is a long way off, and the Old Colony Railroad
runs only to Barnstable as yet; and Mehetabel Rogers
lives below Chatham, on old Cape Cod.

Captain Rogers was light-house keeper at Nausett.
There are three lights there to look after; they stand on
a high bluff, at the foot of which washes the Atlantic,
while back of it stretches a sandy plain, the greater part
of which is yet " Congress land," which our Uncle Sam-
uel does not find it easy to sell, even at a shilling an acre.
Captain Rogers was a sailor, that you might see at the
first glance. He was a ship captain, not a militia captain; that is to say, he had been a ship captain, now he
was a shore captain, and his lights were his ship. It made
little difference to him, so far as responsibility went, or
work either; for though he had no longer a lee-shore to

fear for himself, every easterly gale made him fidget at
his lights, thinking of the poor fellows who might be
warned off by their gleam; and for the rest, his observa-
tions, which were formerly taken at noon, were now made
at midnight; where he would before have got a pull
on the main-sheet, he now ordered a rub of the lantern-
glasses; and if he had no dead-reckoning to work up, he
yet kept a log, no light job to an old tar whose fingers
are handier at a long splice or a timber hitch than at
pot-hooks and hangers.

Captain Rogers was a man of regular habits, for you
see, a light-house keeper is·a responsible person. He is
not like a Governor of a State, or a member of the Cab-
inet, who has all night in, and has only to sign letters, and
order things to be done which are of no consequence
when they are done. A light-house keeper must keep
his lights bright, and if he should be a careless person,
or a sleepy-head, or, perhaps, even a lover of strong drink,
don't you see, some night a poor mariner, steering for his
light in fullest confidence, would run his ship ashore, and
perhaps lose his crew as well as his cargo. From which
you will quickly gather that only the most trusty men
in the State ought to be appointed light-house keepers,
and a man who could not be elected hog-reeve in his
town ought to be ashamed of himself for asking the Sec-
retary of the Treasury, who knows no better, poor ignorant creetur! to trust him with a light.

I advise you not to ask Captain Rogers if he could be
elected hog-reeve. That is beside the matter.

"I wish you warn't goin' to Boston," said the Captain,

for the twentieth time, on the evening of the day before
Aunt Mehetabel was to set out. She was packing up,
and it made him nervous to see now one thing and then
another, now a comb, and then a piece of molasses cake,
and then a pair of stockings, slipped into the carpet-sack
which was to accompany the good lady on her journey.

"Too late," said she, catching up a hymn-book, which
her eye happened to light upon just then, and putting it
into a handy pocket in the all-containing bag, by way of
light reading.

"Seems to break up every thin' so," groaned Uncle
Rogers. "I don't see what's the use of Boston."

"You ain't goin'," was the triumphant reply, as a shiny
and well-preserved pair of shoes were hauled out of a corner and crammed into the bag.

Aunt Mehetabel was determined not to be vexed with
the old man. She was going to Boston; she was sure
of that, and why should she lose her temper? "Men is
sich poor, helpless creeturs. Ef they don't hev every
thin' jest so, they'm all upsot, 'nd no more use 'n a cod-
hook without a bait."

"Now then, old man, there's the ile, and there's the
wick, 'nd there's yer cloths for the lanterns, 'nd there's
the gal, she knows how to cook 's well 's her marm. Now
then, let's turn in, for you've got to drive me over to the
stage soon 's you put out your lights in the mornin'."

The gal's name was Rachel, and she was pretty. There
are a good many pretty girls on old Cape Cod; a Cape
man once told me in confidence that in all his voyages
he had not seen such women as they breed on the Cape,

and I think he was right. Rachel was not only pretty; she could cook, as her mother said; she could iron a shirt, and wash it too; she knew how to clean the lantern-glasses, all except the last finishing touch, which the old Captain administered himself, with a cloth locked up in a separate locker.

Rachel was "hangin' round the room," her mother said, "'s though she expected a feller." Poor child! her "feller" was in Boston, getting ready for a voyage to the Bank Querau after cod; and Rachel was "hangin' round" in hopes that she might, at the last moment, gain permission of her mother to go along in the stage to-morrow.

Aleck Nickerson was captain of the *Lucy Ann,* banker; and the *Lucy Ann* was getting her outfit in Boston for an early start to the Banks. Captain Aleck was determined to fish for "high line" out of Chatham; it was his first voyage as master, and he was what they call a "fishy man"—not a man given to incredible stories, but one who meant to fill his ship, or to "wet his salt," as they say.

He had selected a good crew, and his brother was his mate. Down in Chatham, people said that the *Lucy Ann* was likely to come home with a good stint of fish.

It used to puzzle the gossips which of the two it was that Rachel Rogers favored, whether Aleck, or Mulford his brother. I am not sure that she knew herself. Aleck had committed the indiscretion of almost offering himself to her; and her mother had been rash enough to say once that Aleck Nickerson was a "likely feller;" which makes me think that Mulford had the best chance just then. But the two were always together; and some people pretended to say that they went courting in common, and that either would have been satisfied with the other's success.

"Cape folk" are not cold-blooded, but they are careful. There is an old rule, never to dance with the mate if you can dance with the captain, which is sound enough so far as I know. Some young women, who live by rule, follow this one among others, and I have known them to profit by its observance. In a cold country and a barren, where bread and butter are not over-plentiful, the captain's house has perhaps attractions which the mate's has not; and women, as every body knows, have to live a great deal in-doors. But where promotion goes by merit the captain is apt to be the better man; and, so being, he has a right to the prettiest girl, which no pretty girl I ever knew would dispute. So that, perhaps, after all, Captain Aleck had the best chance.

Aunt Mehetabel arrived safely in Boston, and at once took charge of the *Lucy Ann's* cabin. She had a plan to talk over with Captain Aleck, a plan which had occurred to her during her last visit to Harwich. At this time the gradual failure of the fish, and the somewhat rapid increase of the population of the Cape, caused a good deal of uneasiness to the people of that thrifty region. All the young men and most of the old fellows are fishermen; the whole living of the Cape is taken from the ocean. Hitherto there had been abundance for all, according to their frugal expectations; but now the prospect grew dark. The great fish days off Chatham

H 2

were no longer what they had been in former years.
The fleet, which was formerly always " hauled up " before
Thanksgiving Day, now cruised anxiously after the missing schools till far into December, and could not find
them; and the Banks no longer furnished codfish in the
wonted abundance. And yet every Cape boy is a born
sailor and fisherman. They are a web-footed race; and,
to add to the difficulty, a curiously home-loving race.
Any other people would have emigrated. The California
and Oregon coasts yield fish in such abundance as no
Cape man ever even dreamed of, and to a sailor the world
is open. But to these curious Cape men there is no place
in the world so beautiful or so dear as their own flat,
sandy, tide-washed waste, where the corn scarcely grows
breast-high, and the sand is ankle-deep in the best cultivated garden. Once Uncle Shubael Robbins drove me
out in his hay-wagon, and coming to a knoll a little higher
and a little greener than the surrounding flats, the enthusiastic old fellow cried out, in great exultation, "Let
us stop here and look around: far 's you 've travelled, I
know you never saw so fine a piece of country as this!"
Place him where you will, in the most fertile and beautiful part of the globe if you please, and the Cape Cod man
will sigh wearily for his sand, his pine needles, and the
moan of the ocean on his flat beach. That is in the nature of the creature, and you can not change it.

Given, then, that no one would move away; that all
were bent on fishing; that, in fact, this was the only possible employment for the mass of the people, the single
source of their prosperity; and finally that there were

not fish for all the fishermen : and you will understand that the old folks began to fear a famine for the next generation, and to talk drearily of the fading glories of the Cape.

Just at this time an ingenious Yankee invented the cranberry culture, and saved the Cape. The cranberry is a fruit which grows best on swamp lands which can be overflowed at will with fresh water. It is an amphibious berry, which dwindles and becomes diseased if deprived of an occasional soaking. It is a God-send therefore to a people living in the midst of fresh-water ponds, and a third of whose land lay in worthless swamp, dear at a dollar an acre, useless to all, and owned only because it was a part of the place.

Enoch Doane read about cranberry swamps in his agricultural paper, saw that the berries were in good demand in the Boston market, made a careful calculation overnight, and next morning rode out and bought a dozen acres of the worst-looking swamp land in the neighborhood of Harwich. It took him a year to prepare a ten-acre lot. He had to cut drains, to build proper flood-gates, to clear the land of the rank growth of scrub oak which covered it, to cart away a foot deep of the sour top earth, to carry on new soil, to cover that with a layer of white beach sand, and lastly to set out his berries. He laid out three hundred dollars on each acre of his "patch," and the neighbors united to call him a fool. In three years he was a rich man, swamp lands were worth fifty dollars per acre, and the Cape was saved from starvation.

Now Aunt Mehetabel had heard of Enoch Doane's folly, which was in every body's mouth. She knew he was a shrewd old fellow; and one day she rode down to Harwich in the stage to inspect his operations. She came back the next day in a fluster, and before she ate her dinner had selected the site for a cranberry patch of her own.

The question was, how to raise money enough to.get a couple of acres under cultivation. The old light-house keeper had money in bank; but he plainly told his wife he meant to keep it there; if Enoch Doane was a fool he was not; every body knew that cranberries would presently be worth no more in Boston than beach plums; and then where would all the dollars be which silly people buried in swamps! Fortunately for Aunt Mehetabel the berry fever had not yet got so far down as Nausett, and she was able to buy her two acres of well selected but tangled swamp for little more than a song. Her own savings, from knitting socks, and entertaining chance strangers, were sufficient for that. But how to get it into cultivation? How to clear it of that mass of scrub oak and rank stringy grass which now made it an impregnable fortress? How to pay for drains, and flood-gates, for the much digging, and carting, and hoeing, and planting, which must precede a crop? Captain Aleck Nickerson had a little money in bank, and from him, as one of her nearest neighbors and confidential friends, she resolved to get help. All winter she had done her best to infect him with her own enthusiasm; and now she had come to Boston to make a last effort with him.

"Ef I had jist five hundred dollars I'd hev the pesky

swamp all cleared and sot out before you cum back with your first fare," said she.

"But I want to build my house, Aunt Mehetabel," replied the Captain.

"Ye hain't got nobody to put in it, Aleck."

"Never you mind about that," retorted the Captain with a smile; "how's Rachel?"

"Rachel's ready to wait," said she. "Besides, you haven't asked her."

"Wait till I come back, high line," said Aleck, smiling.

"By that time I can hev the patch clear 's the palm o' yer hand."

"You won't get your money back in three year."

"But the first crop 'll build you two housen, Aleck."

"I don't want but one, old lady, and a pooty gal to live in it."

"You young fellers is always thinkin' 'bout pooty gals. I swan, ef I was a man I'd think o' somethin' else."

"Cranberries, Aunt Mehetabel?" queried Captain Aleck, who was lazy and inclined to tease, and besides owed a grudge to the old woman because she had left Rachel at home.

"Yes, cranberries," she replied; "cranberries is wuth ten dollars a berril, 'nd 'n acre 'll yield fifty berrils easy."

"And the worms 'll eat 'em before ye pick 'em," said Aleck.

"And yer wife 'll git cross 'nd ugly," said Aunt Mehetabel.

"And half crazy 'bout cranberry swamp," said Aleck,

with an irrepressible chuckle, swinging himself suddenly
from the transom, where he was lying, through the open
sky-light on deck.

"You'm a fool, Aleck Nickerson!" screamed the old
woman after him. "O Lordy, what fools men be! Here,
you boy, ye lazy hound, split some wood quick: here's
ten o'clock, 'nd no dinner on the fire. See 'f I don't
worry him into it!" she grumbled to herself, as she poured a mess of beans into the pot.

Captain Aleck "had more 'n half a mind to do it," as
he said to himself. But "better look twice before you
jump once;" and he went into the hold and began to
roll salt barrels and water barrels about, and help stow
the ship for her voyage, "so's to kind o' settle down his
idees."

It is unnecessary to recount the further strife between
these two; the reader already knows, if he has a proper notion of what an ambitious middle-aged woman
can do if she once sets her heart upon a matter, that
Aunt Mehetabel won the battle. The Captain was not
averse to the speculation; he had five hundred dollars
laid aside on interest; he had no doubt of the success
of the enterprise. Cranberries were a "sure thing," as
he well knew. The difficulty was here: he had determined to build himself a house that fall; the place was
chosen and already bought; and he intended that while
the house was building he would court Rachel Rogers,
and when it was finished he would marry her and stay
at home that winter, as he could easily afford to do if he
had only moderate luck on the Banks. The prospect

was an alluring one; like most of the enterprising young fellows on the Cape, he had been going "south," that is to say, to the West Indies, or the Brazils, or Demerara, or Mobile, every winter, to make up the year's work; and the thought of staying at home, in a snug house of his own, all winter, with a pretty young wife, while other fellows were freezing their fingers and toes on the coast, or toiling among molasses hogsheads or cotton bales in the South, was one not lightly to be given up. But "you must keep on the right side of your mother-in-law—at least till you marry your wife," says an old Cape proverb; and Captain Aleck gave way, and made up his mind to go another, and perhaps another winter South, and build his house the grander when the cranberries came in. As he sailed out of the harbor Aunt Mehetabel stood on the dock, her precious bank bills tightly clutched in her hand.

"Remember us both to Rachel, Auntie," said Aleck, pointing toward his brother on the forecastle, "and don't lose the ribbon I sent her;" and so they sailed off for the Banks.

I would not like to have been one of the poor fellows whom Aunt Mehetabel employed to work on her cranberry patch. She looked after them sharply. She did not spare her own hands from the toil, and you may be sure no one else was spared. Even the old Captain was induced to devote his spare hours to the work, which went on rapidly, though slowly enough to the old woman's eager temper. She was determined to surprise Captain Aleck on his return; and before the end of July the whole two-acre lot was cleared and fenced, and a small part of it was already of that strange unearthly white which surprises and disgusts one who sees for the first time a Cape Cod cranberry plantation.

The drains were neatly cut, the flood-gates securely built, and before the autumn frosts she hoped to have the whole ground in readiness for planting.

"Miss Rogers is a hard boss," grumbled the two men who cleared, and dug, and carted fresh earth on to this waste; but "Miss Rogers" was a general who led her troops, and looked very sharply after skulkers.

II.

Meantime, while Rachel cooked, and washed, and ironed, and kept house like a well-trained Cape girl, the *Lucy Ann* was fast anchored on the Banks, and her brace of lovers were such unsightly objects, covered with fish gurry, clad in oil-skins, stamping about in huge sea-boots, and enveloped in barvil and sou'wester and awkward fish-mittens, that she would scarcely have recognized them.   There are Sundays on fish-ground, when all hands shave, and wash, and clean-shirt themselves—if the weather happens to be fine, that is to say.   But if it is rough, a pipe and an old novel and the warm bunk in the cabin are preferred; and the most that is done to renovate the outer man is to wash in warm water and wrap in clean rags the sore fingers which a good fish day produces.

Aleck Nickerson was commonly a lucky man; he

struck fish if any body did. He lifted his anchors less often than most men; and he had a crew that could catch fish if any were within reach of their skillfully con-trived baits. But this time his usual luck seemed to for-sake him. He dropped his cod-lead in vain; "picking fishing," one fish in an hour, and small at that, was the best which fell in his way. Nothing is so disheartening as poor luck in fishing; men lose even their skill, as their confidence oozes out at their fingers' end; and it is only the most sagacious who have the wit to keep their temper, and saw their lines on the rail with the patience which is sure to win in the end.

One day Captain Aleck anchored and struck fish; but not in such abundance as he desired.

"I'll go down in the boat; lower away there, two or three of you," said he, at last. "I'll try 'em a little way off; it's clear weather."

The day was almost cloudless, as fair and smooth as a calm June day off Sandy Hook. The boat was lowered, and Captain Aleck jumped into it with a bucket full of good baits and his codcraft, and pulled away about a mile off, where he had no sooner dropped his lead than he got a bite. The men on board watched him, greedily, for half an hour, sawing their own lines the while across the rail, when, suddenly, they too "struck a school," and in a moment every man was hauling in a twenty pound-er. The Captain was forgotten in the excitement, until the cook chanced to stick his head out of the companion-way, who cried out, "Why, it's as thick as mush!"

So it was. The treacherous fog had settled down all

at once, as it often does on the Banks; and where a short half-hour ago all was clear as a bell, now you could not see the jib-boom end. " Where's the Skipper? " was the question, as all hands held up a moment and stared in each other's faces.

"Ring the bell, quick, some one!" said Mulford. " Skipper's all right, he'll be along soon 's he hears the sound." Nevertheless, Mulford went forward himself, and with an iron belaying-pin beat lustily on the fluke of the spare anchor.

" Hold up a minute," he said, presently ; "listen, every body !" The men stopped talking and bent their ears to the rail; but they heard no plashing of oars, no shout through the white darkness.

"Shout; sing out all together, now !" ordered Mulford. They "sung out" from full throats; then listened again, eagerly, for an answering cry, but none came.

" Ring the bell there, somebody, and ring loud," said Mulford ; " he'll be here, directly."

Somebody rung, and somebody beat the anchor, while another man climbed to the mast-head, to see if he could peer above the fog, and perhaps beyond it; but he came down shaking his head, and declaring that it was thicker up there than down on deck.

Mulford slid down on the dolphin-striker and stretched his head along the surface of the ocean, hoping to get a glimpse in that way, but in vain.

" Sh—sh!" said Uncle David Meeker, suddenly ; " I heard a cry." In a moment all was still, and presently there came a wail ; but it was from the mast-head, and was the lonely voice of a sea-bird welcoming the companionship of man in the thick fog.

"It's only a gull," said some one.

"Good God, this is dreadful! Shout again, men; sing out loud, every man. What would mother say if she was here?" muttered Mulford.

They shouted again and again; they rung the bell and beat the anchor; they listened as men listen on whose hearing depends the life of a shipmate.

"How did the boat bear?" asked the cook.

"Nor-north-east," was the reply. "Let's up anchor and look after him; may be he laid to his line when the fog come up."

"Not yet," was Mulford's reply; "he might have drifted apast us, and then we'd be leaving him."

But now the wind began to sigh through the shrouds, and the little *Lucy Ann* began to roll with the swell which foretold an approaching gale. Her crew looked at each other with solemn faces. In such a fog, once miss the direction, once get out of ear-shot, and the chances are slim of ever finding your ship again.

They went to the windlass presently and hove out the anchor, set the mainsail and jib, and cruised about, making short tacks through the fog, and shouting and listening by turns. All hands remained on deck; the cook in vain cried out, "Sate ye, one half"—the customary call to dinner on a Cape fishing schooner; the dinner was put away untasted; the growing anxiety for their Captain kept every man at his post. The fog did not lift; it began to drive, thick and fast, as the north-east wind blew up; and presently the swash of the sea against the bows became so loud as to make any cry of a human voice inaudible. Then night came on, and at last, after running half a dozen miles dead to leeward, the anchor was let go, a double watch set, and the remainder of the crew went below to their berths in silence.

And thus Captain Aleck was lost to the *Lucy Ann.* To lose a man at sea, and that man the Captain, the leader of the small band, casts a gloom over the whole voyage. Mulford was a capable fellow, he knew the fish-ground as well as his brother; and by a curious turn of luck, when the north-easter blew itself out, the cod seemed to seek the little vessel whose master was drifting no one knew whither or how. The men drew in their fish in silence; the wonted joke was omitted; and every body heaved a sigh of relief when at last, in three weeks after the loss of Captain Aleck, the last barrel of salt was wet, the anchor was hove up for the last time, and all sail set to a fair wind for home.

And now came the most wretched days for Mulford. In the hurry of fishing, and the anxiety of caring for the vessel, his mind had been too fully occupied to leave space for thought about his brother. But now, with a fair wind to fill the sails, and no labor except to work up his reckoning, he began to think, for the first time, that he was to be the bearer of ill-news—and such ill-news. How should he tell the mother who was living quietly and happily at home, waiting in confidence for her son's return, proudly thinking of him as smartest and best among the young men on her "shore" or neighborhood? How should he go to Rachel alone—he who had never visited her except in company with Aleck?

And yet it was pleasant to think that now he might win Rachel for himself. He hated himself for the thought—and yet he thought it. You can not help thinking, that's the mischief of it; and in the midst of the most real sorrow this ugly ray of comfort obtruded itself till poor Mulford, half-distracted, wished the girl at the deuce, whose pretty face made him indulge in a thought which was mean, as he felt, and which had no proper place in his grieving heart. So long as Aleck lived Mulford had been content that Rachel should be his sister-in-law; it was not till now it occurred to him that she could be his own wife. Why not? and yet, why? Should he take advantage by his brother's death? Could he ever forgive himself the joy of such a wedding?

Mulford was not the first generous-hearted man tormented by such thoughts of unwelcome compensations for a great sorrow. And yet how unreasonable, said a voice in his heart. What is done is done; Aleck was lost: should he, for a punctilio, cast away what he felt would be a happiness for him? Should he leave to some stranger that which Aleck would have most certainly preferred him to have, under the circumstances? Was he not his brother's heir? He would inherit his savings —why not also the wife of his heart?

III.

When Mehetabel Rogers heard the news she was "thrown all in a fluster," according to her own account. "What'll Miss Nickerson do?" she cried. "What'll Rachel say, poor gal? O Lordy, what'll become of the cranberry patch?"

This last question was the most important. She had given a summer to that barren swamp, and now it was a fair, smooth, chalky, ugly, but very promising plain, with ditches run through it, and water ready to cover it. She had spent the enormous sum of four hundred and fifty dollars upon it; and she was scared at the outlay, for whose return she and her partner would have so long to wait. She had thought with dread of the account she would have to give to Aleck, and now she must render this account to Mulford—or perhaps, worse yet, to strangers, executors, lawyers! men who were sure to understand nothing except that a frightful sum of money had been wasted, and no sign of profit appeared.

"May be Aleck was picked up!" she at last exclaimed, ran for her bonnet, and set off for the Widow Nickerson's to communicate her hopeful doubt. The two old women hugged the sweet thought to their hearts, and watched daily for some news of the lost Captain. But no news came; the first-fare men were all in and out again, and no tidings were heard; in Cape Ann no one had seen or heard of a missing boat; the second-fare men got home and fitted out for a fall cruise after mack-

erel. At last it was time to give up Aleck for lost; no
hope remained; and when the last banker was hauled
up for the winter, Mrs. Nickerson put on black and gave
up her boy for lost.

Rachel Rogers, too, was clad in mourning, but under-
neath the black stuff gown there beat a very contented
little heart. So long as the two brothers came courting
together she had had no heart in the courtship. While
Aleck was near she would have surrendered to him, because he was the older of the two, and came with an air
which was that of a man used to have his own way, and
to be helped first. Besides he was nearest to that nest-
building which, in Cape Cod life, as among the birds, precedes the wedding. But as Mulford and Rachel sat together, talking of the brother lost, she began to find her
heart warming to the brother living; and their common
sorrow opened the way to a common confidence of love.

When Aleck was given up Rachel was promised to
Mulford; and, to Aunt Mehetabel's satisfaction, the
young fellow proved to have great faith in cranberries. He insisted that the plants should be set out that
fall yet; and before the pond froze over the patch had
been flooded. The work was done; and during the winter she rested and was thankful; not only thankful, indeed, but triumphant. She dragged the old Captain
down to see her work; she boasted in his ears of the
bushels of crimson berries which should reward her labors and justify the outlay. She had scarcely patience
to wait till spring.

The spring came; Mulford was off to the Banks in a

new vessel; the swamp was drained, and the cranberries were in bloom; when, one day, Captain Aleck Nickerson walked into his mother's house, sat down on a chair in the kitchen, and said, "How's all at home?"

The poor mother thought at first she saw a ghost, but when she felt her boy's arms around her she fell away in a happy swoon. While Aleck was yet busy with her came in to these two—Rachel Rogers. She gave a little scream of terror when she saw her old lover, and, obeying the first impulse, ran out of the house. But presently she turned and came back. She could not leave Captain Aleck alone with his fainting mother; he needed help; and for the rest—she must see him at some time. But as she walked slowly back to the door, how her heart hardened toward the poor fellow within! "What business had he to come back?" she was saying to herself.

"Glad to see you've come back safe, Captain Nickerson," she said to Aleck as she stepped into the kitchen again.

"All right, Rachel," said he, looking up. "But first let's get the old woman to rights. I hope my droppin' in on her hain't killed her."

The poor old mother presently came to herself. She clung to her son, whom the deep had given up; but as she gathered her thoughts in order, and saw Rachel standing there, with stony face, her joy was distracted by the thought of the changes which a year had produced.

"We thought you were dead, boy," said she, fondly smoothing his hair.

"You see I'm as live as any man of my size and weight," replied Aleck, shaking himself to prove that he was real flesh and blood.

"Go home, Rachel, and tell your mother," said she, dismissing the young girl, who turned and went out silently.

"What's the matter with Rachel?" asked Captain Aleck. "She don't seem glad to see me back."

"She thought you was lost, my son."

"And then?"

"She's promised to Mulford, my son," said the old woman, looking at him anxiously. "But oh, Aleck, I'm so happy! Don't mind her. Look at me. It was so weary without you, boy."

Captain Aleck sat himself down silently in a chair beside her. It was not such a coming home as he had looked forward to.

"Where's Mulford, mother?" he asked, after awhile.

"He's got a new vessel, and he's gone to the Banks."

"Did he do well last year?"

"Yes, he was lucky. He made money. But he grieved for you, Aleck; it was a blow to him."

"And Rachel's promised to him?"

"Yes, boy. But what makes you sit there so solemn? Why don't you look to me? Don't you see I'm glad you've come home?"

Her old eyes filled with tears of longing love. Hard-featured she was, hard-handed, wrinkled, faded, with a harsh, cracked voice—now curiously soft and womanly. She looked at him as though she feared he would fly out

I

of the window; she studied the shadows flitting across his dark face as though her life depended upon his humor.

"Come, sit you down close by me," she said, as he began to walk about the room, and examine the walls and windows, and the dishes in the pantry. "I can't bear you out of my sight, Aleck. What's the use of botherin' about that gal? I'm your mother, that bore you, 'nd nussed you, 'nd kerried you round in my arms. I love you, Aleck; I'm glad you've come home. I've got more right to you than any gal on the Cape."

"Tell me how it was," said she, presently, curious to hear how he was saved from the death which must have been so near him, and ready, too, to divert his mind from poor Rachel.

The story was simple enough. He had been able to keep his little shallop afloat till, late at night, he saw suddenly the huge hull of a ship looming through the fog, and bearing straight down upon him. Unable to get out of her path, death seemed certain. But with a seaman's presence of mind he saw his opportunity; with a seaman's eye he measured the distance for a leap for life; and as the vast hull swept down upon his cockleshell he jumped for her dolphin-striker, caught it, and was saved. Twice he was dipped in the ocean as the ship pitched her bows under the sea-way. But at last he clambered to the bowsprit, and in on deck, where he had hard work to persuade the superstitious French crew not to throw him overboard, so scared and amazed were they at his appearance. The ship was a French Indiaman, carrying a cargo of fish to Pondicherry. The captain set him off upon a homeward-bound American ship in the Indian Ocean. And here he was, with nearly a twelvemonth lost out of his life, as he said.

"But you're saved to your old mother," said she.

"And Rachel Rogers is promised to Mulford?" said Captain Aleck.

"You mustn't think hard on her, Aleck; gals don't know much—and she thought you was gone."

"Was it so long to wait?" he asked, conscious that he would have waited twice a twelvemonth for her.

"Mehetabel was willin', and Rachel didn't know which she liked best of you two, Aleck. You always went courtin' in couples."

"It's not too late to go to the Banks yet," he said, thinking aloud. "I can go down to Provincetown to-morrow, and get a pinky for myself."

"Not so soon, Aleck; not so soon, boy; I want you a little while. I want to look at you, to see how you've growed."

"Lord a-massy! and so you've come back, Aleck Nickerson!" shouted Aunt Mehetabel, coming into the kitchen; "glad to see ye alive! The cranberries is all in: won't you come over and look at the swamp?"

"I'm goin' to Provincetown to-morrow to look up a vessel fit to go to the Banks," said Captain Aleck. "I dare say the cranberries'll keep.

"But I can't; I've got my work to show you, and the swamp belongs to ye till you get your money back, Aleck."

"Never mind, Aunt Mehetabel, I don't want to build my house now."

"For why don't ye? Don't look grouty the first time I see ye; I'll be sorry about the money I owe ye."

Poor Aleck was sadly badgered with these women. He had expected to come home and find Miss Rachel receive him as a lover lost and found; he heard only about cranberry swamps. He had never thought about her except as his own, and yet he vexed himself with the thought that his own ill-luck, and not Rachel, was in fault; and that his ill-humor was neither manly, nor fair to her who caused it, or to his poor old mother, who was sad on his account when she ought to have been entirely happy.

"I'll send my old man over for you by and by, Aleck," said Aunt Mehetabel, feeling—the crafty old woman—that she was not likely just yet to get a good word from him.

"I'm a mean fool to be puttin' on a sour face, mother, about this gal," said Aleck, looking up after she was gone. "It'll be all right when I see Mulford once. Better let me go off to-morrow. This 'll all wear off when I get on fish ground again."

He rode over to Provincetown in the stage next morning; found a little pink-sterned schooner laid up, which no one had thought worthy of another trip to the Banks; hauled her up, cleaned her bottom, painted it in two tides, picked up a crew, got his outfit, and in a week was on the way to the region of fogs and fish. Before he sailed he visited the lights, and to Aunt Mehetabel's great delight expressed his satisfaction at the condition of the cranberry patch. Also he met Miss Rachel, who held out her hand to him, like a girl who bears no grudge against a discarded lover—a piece of generosity which not many young women are capable of.

"I'm goin' to look up Mulford, Rachel; take care of yourself till I bring him home," he said. His heart was light once more; a week of hard work, and a foretaste of the Banks, had set his thoughts in order. "I felt mean to ye at first, Rachel," he said, as they walked out together toward the road; "but it warn't your fault, gal. And Mulford's a good fellow as ever lived."

So he sailed away.

One day his little vessel lay pitching like a mad bull, in a north-easterly gale, with all her cable out and a rag of storm-sail fluttering in the gale, while in the high stern sat Skipper Aleck, with two or three weather-beaten fishermen in sou'westers and oiled-clothes, watching the weather. The sea was too heavy to fish, and the fog was so thick that a good lookout was necessary.

"When it broke away awhile ago I saw a vessel off yonder, to windward," said David Meeker; "'t looked like Mulford's schooner, too. Had jist sich a kink in her topmast. But I couldn't see her but for a minute; may be 't warn't."

"Anchored?" asked the Skipper.

"No; onder way. Dreffle work to be onder way sich weather."

"Too thick to bang about much," said Sylvie Baker. "I'd ruther lay to anchor than onder sail."

"We'll have to look out for that fellow, boys," said Aleck, cheerfully. "Hope he'll not foul our hawse."

"Guess he stood across, on the starboard tack; he's all clear before this."

"Whew! how it howls!" said Sylvie Baker, as a squall burst fiercely over the little vessel, and for a moment bore her down, and held her and the sea almost still.

Just then the fog bank lifted a little, and the alert eyes of the little group peered curiously around, as the vessel rose on a great sea, in search of possible companions.

"By gracious! how wild it looks — hello! what's that?" shouted one, pointing directly to windward, where now only a great black mass of water was to be seen as the schooner sank with a receding billow. "That's a wreck, ef my old eyes is wuth any thin'."

All hands watched eagerly. It was quite a minute before the vessel was thrown up on a sufficiently high sea to enable them to get a fair view. Then all cried, with one voice, "A wreck! a wreck!"

"Turn out there, boys!" cried Skipper Aleck down the companion-hatch; "this fellow 'll be down on top of us if he don't mind!"

The sleepers tumbled out of their warm berths, and crawled into their oiled jackets and fish-boots as hurriedly as they could. It was unwelcome news which the Skipper had cried down the hatch, and some who were dressing themselves in the cabin were pale at the thought of it. Leave them alone, and they were safe, there in the midst of the ocean, with a fierce north-easter blowing great guns, and the sea rolling mountains high —safe as though they had been sleeping with their wives at home. Let the wind howl; let the sea bellow, and hiss, and tumble their little cockle-shell about, as though it was bent now on dashing her on the sand a hundred fathoms down below, and again tossing her up to the pale full moon, of which they got a glimpse over-head once in a while. Their cable was new and strong; their little sharp-sterned craft was of a build to outride many a line-of-battle ship; only leave them alone, and these accustomed seamen ate their cold cut of beef and slept in their narrow berths as securely as any Wall-Street banker in his Fifth Avenue mansion. But once slip the cable; once derange, in the middle of such a gale, the conditions on which their comfort and safety depended, and they knew that they would have such a struggle with the storm as not one but dreaded—such a battle for life as none of them could be sure of winning in.

The vessel which was drifting down upon them was about two miles away when she was first seen. She was dismasted; her mainmast was a mere stump; her fore-mast was swept away flush with the deck. She was tossed about like a helpless chip, a bit of rag fluttering from the stump of the mainmast barely sufficing to keep her head to the wind. Captain Aleck and his crew watch-ed her with eager and careful eyes. It was only at intervals they got a momentary glimpse of her. The sea ran so high that it was only when both vessels happened to be at the same time tossed upward, and when no intermediate mountain roller obstructed the sight, that they could see the helpless, dismasted craft.

"She's not anchored, Skipper," shouted David Meeker into Aleck's ear.

"No, she's drifting down on us," replied Aleck, looking nervously forward, where a few flakes of his stout hempen cable still lay faked neatly on the deck—too few to be of use in getting out of the way of the approaching vessel.

"We can't stick out any more; there ain't enough," shouted David, in answer to his Captain's glance.

"She's going to leeward like mad; looks 's though she'd fetch agin us, sure."

The discipline of a fishing vessel is not very strict. The men obey the captain, but they know as much as he does, and they do not always wait for orders. Every man aboard understood the necessities of the case perfectly, and it did not need Skipper Aleck's orders to set them to reefing the mainsail and foresail.

"Balance reef's the best, Skipper?" roared some one, making himself understood as well by signs.

Aleck nodded; and the sails were so reefed that only a small triangular piece of each would be exposed if it became necessary to raise them.

"Lash down the throat solid," shouted the Skipper. "Don't let any thing get adrift—look out!" as a great sea swept under the schooner, and flung her for a moment nearly straight on end. The cook's tin pans rattled drearily in the galley—a sound which those who have heard it in a great storm at sea never forget. It strikes the ears of seamen as a sign of the utmost violence of a gale.

The men at the sails were swung off their feet, and clung to the rigging with their hands till she settled down again. Those in the high stern used the moment when they were tossed up to watch the fast-approaching wreck.

" She comes down on us awful fast," said Uncle David.

She was not more than half a mile away now. She had drifted a full mile in seven or eight minutes; the sea and wind were sweeping her along at the rate of not less than eight knots an hour. In less than five minutes more it would be decided whether Captain Aleck's little *Swallow* was safe or no.

" Go forward now with your axe, Uncle David; don't cut till I tell ye, old man; and stand clear when ye cut. Sylvie Baker, stand by the foresail and keep yer eye on me. Tell the boys to lash themselves fast. Drive half a dozen nails into this companion slide here; if we ship a sea it may wash it off else, and fill the cabin."

" She not a dozen ship's lengths off now, Skipper," said Job Scudder, pointing with his finger at the schooner, on whose deck a few helpless mites could by this time be seen clinging to the bulwarks and motioning, as though dumbly entreating them for help. There was no longer any fog to obscure the vision. The blinding spoon-drift swept constantly across, impelled with such

I 2

violence by the fury of the gale that it struck the face
like needle-points or like sharp hail. The sea was white
with foam, and the tops of the huge black mountain billows curled over in foam rifts, which broke with a hoarse,
sullen roar, and were swept by or under the *Swallow*
with a dull hiss, as of ten thousand venomous serpents
eager for the lives of the crew. At such times the
waves no longer appear sea-green; their vast masses,
rolled up by the steady fury of the wind, are dark and
gloomy, as though laden with a thousand deaths; they
have a resistless weight and momentum; they move
with the same majestic grandeur which distinguishes and
makes awful the great tide which rolls over the Canadian
fall at Niagara. They break slowly, and the curling top
of such a wave is instantly seized by the wind and dashed, in sheets of fiercely-driven drops, along the surface:
this is called "spoon-drift."

As the dismasted hull swept down toward them, the
crew of the little *Swallow* forgot for a moment their own
peril, in watching eagerly the helpless creatures who
were now so near that their faces could be seen. The
wreck was almost directly ahead. "She'll drift athwart
our cable, sure, and then we're gone," old David was saying to himself, while all held their breath in dread sus-
pense. Just then, when their own fate seemed already
sealed, a huge wave seized the hulk and carried her in
one great bold sweep down past the *Swallow's* bow. As
both vessels rose on the high crest of a sea they lay for
a moment abreast, and not twenty yards apart, and the
two crews scanned eagerly each other's faces.

"Good God! it's your brother Mulford, Skipper!" roared the cook, who stood at Captain Aleck's side, clinging to the same shroud, and pointing to a figure, with flying hair and sea-washed clothes, which was lashed to the quarter of the wreck.

Captain Aleck had seen him already; he stood, pale and silent, looking with scared eyes at the vision, which lasted but a moment. In the next the vessel was hidden by an intervening wave; but as she disappeared a cry of mortal terror came from her crew—a cry so sharp, so full of horror that it pierced through the roaring gale, and reached even to the ears of the *Swallow's* men. Well might they cry out, the hapless crew; for, with death clutching at them in every wave, they saw suddenly before their eyes the apparition of one whom the seas had swallowed up a year ago, as they believed—they saw Captain Aleck Nickerson standing there, one risen from the dead, to call them to a fate like his own.

"They've gone down!" screamed David, who had worked his way aft again; he understood the cry they had heard as the last utterance of the drowning wretches.

"Not yet—there they drift," shouted Aleck, who had leaped up on the top of the main gaff, and held himself there by the throat halyards. "There they drift, poor fellows! We can't help them now; they're too far off."

He comprehended well enough the meaning of the cry which had come from Mulford and his crew; he waved wildly with his arms toward the fast-disappearing hulk, eager to assure the poor fellows that he was no spirit summoning them to death; but his motions, if they saw them, were not calculated to re-assure.

IV.

The gale blew itself out that night; and a sharp rain, which set in for some hours toward morning, cut down the sea so much that when the sun rose, bright and cheery, and the blue sky was once more seen, all hands were quickly called to weigh anchor and set sail in search of the wreck. Aleck buckled on his spy-glass and mounted to the main cross-trees, to look out. The wind blew lightly from the southward, and as they sailed slowly along half the crew gathered in the cross-trees and rigging, every eye scanning the horizon for some sign of the wreck. For many hours they saw nothing; but about two o'clock in the afternoon Captain Aleck, who had tasted no food yet that day, nor felt the need of any, in his anxiety for his brother, sung out sharply, "Look out on the starboard bow there; I think I see a spar or something floating."

"Keep her away a point," he ordered the helmsman presently, when he had viewed the object through his glass.

As they bore down upon it it proved to be a mast, but no live thing was attached to it.

"That belongs to some one else than Mulford. It warn't lost in this gale; see the barnacles on it," said one of the men before they came up to it.

"Haul her up again!" ordered Captain Aleck.

But presently they came to other signs of shipwreck—floating barrels, a bucket, part of a stove boat; and at last, in the far distance, sharp-eyed David declared he saw a spar, with something like a flag waving.

"It's only the sea breaking over it," said the Skipper, nervously, not daring to give his hopes an airing in words; yet he watched intently the piece of wreck toward which the *Swallow* was now sailing. Certainly there was something like a fluttering rag visible on it as it was lifted by the swell; and what was that black thing which clung to the spar? "I do believe there's a man on that wreck!" shouted Captain Aleck, suddenly, in some excitement. "Here, David, take a careful look with the glass."

"He's waving to us," said David, after some minutes. "It's a man. I see his arms wavin'. Now I see him tryin' to stand up. He sees us plainly. He is on three spars lashed together. He keeps wavin', poor creetur!" This much David reported in a monotonous voice, without removing his eye from the glass.

"Bring up the colors, some of you," ordered Aleck; "we'll let him know we see him, anyhow. Look sharp, there! It's not comfortable waitin' on that spar for a sign from us. Get the boat ready, down there!"

"Boat's all ready, Sir," was the reply.

"O dear, how slow we do go ahead!" fidgeted the Captain at the mast-head. "Seems to me we don't get any nearer at all. There, thank God! he sees the colors. Look, David, he's sot down. Thank the Lord! he's comfortable now, poor fellow!"

"There's more wreck on the lee bow, Skipper!" sung out a man who was perched on the foremast-head. "By Godfrey, there's two men on that piece! I see 'em both. Seems to me one's dead; he don't move."

"Take hold there and launch that boat; I can't wait any longer," cried Aleck, swinging himself from the cross-trees, and sliding rapidly down on deck. "Get in here with me, Tom; it's only a quarter of a mile, and we can pull it easily."

"Keep an eye on the others, aloft there," he ordered, as they struck out from the *Swallow*. "First come first served: they'll have to wait."

The two oarsmen had no easy task before them. The sea was still high. The rain of last night had smoothed the tops of the billows; the waves no longer broke angrily, but there remained the long ground-swell, which takes always some days to subside. The little shell of a boat was not a very safe conveyance; but Skipper Aleck did not think of safety for himself. He and his companion tugged at their oars, now forcing the boat up the great mountain-side of a long wave, and presently propelled with a fearful rush into a deep pit of waters. The wind had nearly died out, and, slowly as they made headway, they progressed more rapidly than the *Swallow*, whose sails were half the time becalmed under the lee of the great seas.

"I'd give all I'll ever be worth ef that was Mulford Nickerson," said Captain Aleck, half to himself. "Pull, Tom Connor; do your best; I want to see the man's face."

It was a long pull; but at last they heard a faint shout, and, turning their heads the next time the boat rose on a swell, they saw the poor fellow whom they came to save.

"All right, my man!" shouted Aleck, in reply. "Look at his face, Tom Connor, and see ef you know him. I can't bear to look."

"It's not your brother, Skipper," reported Tom, in a few minutes. "It's Dan'el Twyer, of Barnstable."

The poor Skipper gave a groan, but pulled ahead. "We'll make his wife glad, anyhow, please God," said he. "Hold fast, Uncle Dan'el!" he shouted; "we'll get you safe aboard directly!"

With skillful management they got the boat alongside the floating spar for a moment, without knocking a hole in her bottom; and in that moment Daniel Twyer, summoning for the effort all the little strength he had left, leaped into the stern sheets, and sank down in a heap, with dazed eyes and a frightened look, asking, "Be you alive, Aleck Nickerson, or be you a sperrit?"

"He's more alive than you, you old fool!" answered Tom Connor, gruffly, ready to quarrel with the poor fellow, now that he had saved his life; "where's your Skipper?"

But Daniel Twyer was too weak to reply; the feeling that he was safe, that presently he would be on a ship's deck, overcame him, and he dropped insensible in the stern sheets, and was not aroused till Connor had put a bow-line under his arms, and he felt himself swung on board, and lying upon the deck of the *Swallow.*

" Keep her away for the other men ! " shouted the Captain, as he leaped on board, and the boat was hauled in over the low rail of the schooner. " Now then, Dan'el Twyer, where's your Skipper ? " he demanded.

" Mulford Nickerson and Zebah Snow was lashed to the main-hatchway when I saw 'em last."

The wind had freshened, and the *Swallow* was running down toward the two men rapidly. David Meeker sat in the cross-trees, with the glass, watching them, and waving his hat every few minutes, to re-assure their hopes.

Presently he sung out, " 'Pears to me one on 'em's Zebah Snow—"

" Hurrah, boys ! " shouted Aleck, his anxious face at last lighted up with joy.

" T'other one's dead," added David.

" 'Tain't so ! " instantly shouted the Skipper in return. " 'Tain't so ; ef he was dead his weight wouldn't cumber the raft." And in a moment he had " shinned " to the cross-trees and held the glass to his own eye.

" 'Tain't so, Uncle David," he repeated ; " you don't know nothin' 'bout it, old man. T'other one's Mulford Nickerson, and he ain't dead, by Godfrey, for—there ! I saw him move ! " he shouted, at the top of his voice. " Get that boat ready to launch, down there on deck ! "

Down he slid, and in a minute was once more afloat in the boat, pulling with eager strokes for the raft, which the *Swallow* dared not approach too nearly for fear of being flung on top of it by the sea.

" Who's that on the hatch with you, Snow ? " he called out, as the boat neared the raft.

The man who had been declared dead tottered half to his feet, but fell again, crying out, "Is it you, Aleck Nickerson?" It was all he could say. The next minute Zebah Snow was jerked off the raft, and flung into the boat, and Captain Aleck stood in his place.

"Thank God, it's you, sure," said he, grasping Mulford's hands in both his; "but what's the matter?"

"My leg's broke in two places. And you're alive, dear old fellow! Thank God for that, anyhow. I don't care now. We thought it was your ghost when we drifted past you in the gale."

They got him on to the boat and into the *Swallow's* cabin as carefully as they could; and here his leg was dressed, and he was cared for as tenderly as rough but kind-hearted seamen knew how. They are a rude set, no doubt, the men of the sea, and have but little pity for the minor ails. They are merciless toward men with headaches, or nerves, or dyspepsia; they can not believe a man sick if he can walk or eat; but there is no tenderer nurse, no more thoughtful, skillful, long-suffering, self-denying attendant on a real and serious sick-bed than the roughest old tar in the forecastle.

When Skipper Aleck had seen Mulford comfortably tucked away in his own berth, and had administered a cup of tea and such other nourishment to him as was fit and at hand, he went on deck and called his crew around him. Codfishermen are not paid wages; each man keeps account of his own fish, and receives their value when they are sold, less a certain share reserved for the owners of the vessel, and another smaller share which the Captain has for his conduct of the voyage. Aleck was determined to steer at once for home; but the *Swallow* was not more than half full of fish, and to make what is called a broken voyage would be a serious loss to men who had families to feed and clothe.

The seniors of the crew had already agreed upon their course, however; and when their Captain said, " Men, I want to take the *Swallow* home as fast as she can sail," David Meeker put the helm up, Tom Connor bent on the stay-sail, and with a ready, " All right, Skipper!" the little craft was put upon her proper course with all sail set.

On the tenth day they ran into Provincetown. It was a bright June day, and Mulford, who had been gradually sinking, lay upon the deck with his brother by him.

" Don't think hardly of poor Rachel," he said, for the hundredth time. " It was I that persuaded her; and God knows I was sorry for you, brother; but we all thought you dead."

" I'll dance at your wedding, dear old fellow, this winter," said Aleck.

" You'll bury me in the old grave-yard next to father," replied Mulford, solemnly; " and, Aleck, promise me that you'll take Rachel. She loves you now; she's a good gal; don't let me go, feelin' that I parted you two."

Aleck held the poor fellow's hot hands in his own. He did not suspect how near his brother was to death.

There was not much pain in the broken leg now; but that was because mortification had set in. The fractured limb had been too badly wounded when it was jammed between two heavy floating spars, to afford hopes of recovery, even had Mulford had more skillful treatment than the poor fishermen could give him. He died shortly after they had cast anchor; and poor Aleck, broken with grief, set out for home to carry the sad tidings to his mother.

It is a true story which I have told you; and the poor mother who sorrowed for two sons lost at sea, and yet thanked God for one of them saved, still lives with that one who now brought home his dead brother. The women of the Cape have need of stout hearts, for they do not know what moment their dearest are suffering the agony of death; they can not tell what minute shall make any one of them a widow or childless. I could show you a row of white houses in a little Cape village, in seven of which live the widows made by one great gale. It is not often the greedy sea gives up its dead; it is not always, alas! that of two sons one is saved; and when the Widow Nickerson had heard all this sad tale it was not without proper cause she said, through her tears, "I've saved one, anyhow. Thank God, who took away, but who also gave me back you, my boy!"

She lives yet, this old woman, and is happy too; for is she not spoiling a white-haired grandson, who, at three years old, is impatient to be six, that he may be cook of his father's schooner?

Rachel and Aleck sorrowed together over Mulford's death. They are now man and wife. Captain Aleck had to "go away South" for a couple of winters to restore his broken fortunes; but with this and two good fish years he gained back more than he had lost. And one Thanksgiving afternoon he went over and asked Rachel if she would marry him.

The cranberry patch in these years had borne so abundantly that Aunt Mehetabel was regarded in her neighborhood as a woman of great capacity and good luck; and when Captain Aleck came to ask her and the old light-house keeper for their daughter, she said, "Rachel's been waitin' for ye, Aleck; she wouldn't hev none else but you—and this year's crop of berries 'll build you yer house."

"The worms 'll eat 'em before you pick 'em," said Aleck, remembering the old bout in the *Lucy Ann's* cabin.

"They'm all picked, and not a worm amongst 'em," she replied. "And ef it warn't for them cranberries you'd hev to go away this winter, little as you thought it, instead of sittin' comfortable in your own house. Tell ye what, boy, cranberry swamp's better 'n goin' to the Banks."

If the respectable reader will accept that last sentence as a moral to this true tale he is welcome to it.

MAUD ELBERT'S LOVE MATCH.

MAUD ELBERT'S LOVE MATCH.

JAMES GRANT landed in New York, in the summer
of 1793, with two suits of clothes, a chest of carpenter's tools, a pair of strong arms, and a stout heart. He
left Aberdeen because he thought to better his condition
in America; and being a shrewd, common-sensible
Scotchman, he found no difficulty in doing so. Discovering himself able to earn bread and butter for two, he
presently sent out for the girl he'd left behind him, and
when she arrived, duly married her, and installed her
mistress of a little house he had meantime built. As
years passed along quietly, James Grant invested the
good woman's savings and his own in a quantity of fa-
vorably-situated country lots, which are now rather below the business centre of the big city which New
Yorkers call the metropolis. In their little house, next
to the carpenter's shop, the old folk lived and died, to
the great disgust of the present head of the family, then
a rising young merchant, who got out of it long ago, and
into a Fifth Avenue palace nineteen and three-quarters'
feet wide, and very high stooped.

This is quite enough of James Grant, whose life, being only a poor devil of a ship-carpenter's, I do not propose to take. He was too unremarkable a man for me to trouble myself or the reader with; I don't believe the poor fellow ever had even a political aspiration in his life, which, however, when you properly consider it, is so strange a fact in the history of an adopted American that it almost entitles him to a critical biography, in the popular style of the Honorable and Reverend O. Phydl, D.D.

J. Augustus Grant is the grandson of old James Grant. I have been told, by one of those disagreeable persons who "recollect" every thing, that in his youth, some three-and-twenty years ago, when the Fifth Avenue palace was yet safely hidden in the brain of the architect, and three generations of Grants hived together in the little house, J. Augustus was popularly known on the street as "Little Jimmy Grant," as mischievous an urchin as ever knuckled down to taw. I admire the taste which dictated the addition and proper prominence of "Augustus." Had he remained only plain Jimmy Grant, I should perhaps never have told this little story of him.

Before James Augustus got fairly into trowsers and boots a great change was made in his life. The country lots having got sufficiently down town to become very valuable, Peter Grant, son of James and father of J. A., induced the old carpenter to sell out, and with the proceeds establish him in business. Peter was a good business man, and before very long time the Fifth Avenue palace was built, and J. Augustus became at once a respectable juvenile, with an aristocratic weakness for trotters—not sheeps' trotters, but livery-stable trotter.

Young America has a very surprising knack at suiting itself to its place in the world. There is scarce a tallow-chandler's son in all Fifth Avenue but bears himself as though his ancestors had lived in palaces since before the flood; and I am sure no one who has seen these "young scions of our aristocracy," as the Jeames of the *Home Journal* prettily calls them, but will perceive at once the justice and sagacity of Mr. Buchanan's remark to the Queen, that the Americans are a nation of sovereigns. J. Augustus, who no sooner got into his papa's palace than he seemed to every one to have been born there, was of course in due time sent to college; where he acquired the proper proficiency in Greek, Latin, and Mathematics, slang, billiards, and brandy smashes. He astonished his "governor" with regularly recurring bills for horse-hire, which persuaded that speculative old gentleman that the keeping of livery stables must be the most lucrative business in the world; and mystified his mother, on his vacation visits home, by insisting on a night-key, and requesting to have his breakfast in bed. She thought at first that Gussy was in feeble health, good soul! and proposed to send up also the family physician. It should be said that the young man graduated with credit to himself. At a subsequent supper he developed political aspirations, and made an astonishing speech on manifest destiny; in which he abused the old fogies, threatened the British Lion, and declared his con-

K

viction that the first duty of every true-born American is to feather the nest of our national bird. His father told him next day that he had made an ass of himself, which made J. A. laugh. The old folks don't understand these things, you see.

To a wealthy American there seem but two paths open; business and—nothing. Of the two, in the present wholesome state of our civilization, the former seems preferable, as being least unendurable. J. Augustus, of course, was not going to waste his life in a profession. Peter was a first-class business man, a China merchant, Grant & Elbert, you might have seen their sign, ay, and their fine, stanch old tea-ships too, any day you chose to stroll down along South Street. So there was an opening made for young Grant, pending which opening he proposed to spend a couple of years in Europe, which to young men of J. A.'s kidney seems to signify chiefly, Paris. I wonder if Abraham's young men made Gomorrah their head-quarters when they went abroad?

On J. A.'s return, which was brought about by his father's refusal to honor his drafts after a certain date, he found the opening ready for him. That it did not exactly suit him was evinced by the fact that he filled it only about once a week, when he drew his pay; spending the remainder of his valuable time* on the road, and at his club—the last a delightful place, where, I am told, young men eat, drink, and talk intelligently about horses and "giurls."

Why should he do differently? Did not all the young

---

* "Time is money."—POOR RICHARD.

men, his social peers, do the same? Why should he make a guy of himself down in South Street, while there was still a bit of life not worn threadbare for him? Was he not his father's sole heir? Was not the governor worth a cool three hundred thousand? And was not this promising youth by and by to marry pretty Maud Elbert with $100,000 more?

Which puts me in mind that I have as yet said nothing about Miss Maud, who, as a young person worth the snug sum aforementioned, and intended by kind Fate to be the heroine of this story, should have been treated with more courtesy. Maud Elbert, may it please you, then, is my heroine, a tall, straight, brown-haired girl, whose acquaintance would tell you she was proud; whose friends thought her only reserved; whose few intimates loved her as the humblest, the cheeriest, the kindest; a girl with a smile like a June morning, but with a power of cool stare in her clear blue eyes, equal, so I have heard J. A. say, to forty brown-stone fronts, a Fifth Avenue figure of speech which I commend to the young gentlemen of the clubs.

I think there are people who somehow feel it a misfortune to be " cradled in the lap of luxury," as the lady novelists nicely style it. There is a kind of mind which wilts in the fierce glare of too great prosperity, and blossoms brightest and fullest in cloudy weather or in shady nooks. I don't say this of myself, or of you, reader, or of J. A. Augustus was little troubled with this weariness of being served, of being " done for " instead of doing, which often brought into Maud's blue eyes that far-gazing, nothing-distinguishing look, that deepest, quietest trouble in an honest eye, which, to the observing, portends a soul rusting in fetters. This was what you might see in Maud. Not unhappiness: why should she be unhappy whose every possible want was ministered to almost before it was felt? But to a true soul thus circumstanced, and especially to a true woman's soul, there are bright possibilities each day perishing in the dim budding, which cast about her whole life this soft tinge of unavailing sorrow. To such

> "Chambers of the great are jails,
> And head-winds right for royal sails."

How far what a woman does often falls short of what she is! And then steps in some stupid satirist, and, applying to her life the remorseless logic of achievement, cries, "Lo! here is one found wanting!" Is there any sight more sadly touching than this of a fair young girl's soul, gold-fettered and condemned by unpropitious Fate to be mastered by servants, by society, by finery, by any and all of the cumbrous, servile trifles which hinder and belittle the development of any true God-given life? What sublime pity must He, who judges as men do not judge, give these, His helpless ones, blindly and wearily struggling against the devouring tide of worldliness.

This Maud Elbert, whom I wish it were given me to place more clearly before your inward eye, had been betrothed to James Augustus Grant these many years; since early childhood indeed, when their fond fathers, having gained in some speculation of unusual hazard and percentage, and feeling the cockles of their hearts warmed toward each other, as do men who have, arm to arm, mastered some great danger—when these fond old shipping merchants, I say, pledged their two smiling innocents to each other, and vowed to secure the present good understanding of the firm with that sacramental cement known as the marriage ceremony. They grew up in the full knowledge of their predestinated union; were accustomed to walk and ride together as little children; quarrelled and made up as boy and girl; and by the time they were full blown into young society-hood, had grown so familiar that they didn't know each other at all, and didn't care for each other a straw. When J. A. went to Europe Maud went also on her travels; not, of course, in the same steamer, nor even in the same general direction; though they did meet in Paris, where J. A. dutifully divided himself between Maud and a French friend whose acquaintance he had made at the Jardin Mabille. When J. A. returned Maud was the beauty of her set, which, of course, pleased him. Why shouldn't it? Was not she to be his wife by and by? And don't a man like to see his wife, or fiancée, admired, within bounds? Pleased him the more, that it was evident, even to his dull and careless vision, that, if she cared no great deal for him, she loved no one better. Why should she? In her set J. A. was not more useless or worse than any of the others; and he certainly danced more elegantly than some. And out of her set?

Pray, did you ever know a young girl with $100,000 marry out of her set?

And marrying, you know, is the chief business of life. Prudent mammas fondly hope to rescue the morals of imprudent sons by an early marriage. Prudent papas speculatively think to make the fortunes of imprudent sons by a wealthy marriage. Prudent sons regard the transaction with a business eye, and hope to gain out of it larger means and greater liberty. And the bride? God help her! Except, as sometimes happens, she is able to help herself.

The match which had been so conveniently arranged for these young people seemed in every respect felicitous, except, perhaps, in the matter of love. But then it is to be considered that love had not been in the minds of the projectors; though in such matters love is oftener the cause than the effect. So far, however, as appeared to the world, or indeed to the thoughts of the two most interested, the affair was settled. Maud Elbert did not give her mind to a future so mapped out for her. Your fatalist is never a reasoning being; and indolent people scarce care to waste a thought upon those affairs which God, or fate, or fortune, seem to have placed out of their control. And J. A.? J. A. drew his weekly allowance out of the opening so conveniently provided for him in South Street, and having now pretty much run through his limited range of life, took to reading, and misunderstanding, Thackeray, and tried to do the cynical: a kind of Diogenes the Magnificent, snarling at society out of his gilded tub on the edge of Fifth Avenue, and making sarcastic comments on the way of life of those who spend more than $20,000 a year.

It is the fashion to rail at the money-getting spirit of us Americans; but money-getting is better than nothing-getting. To speculate in Wall or South Street is at least exercise for the mind, and though the male intellect might be applied to better purposes, happy he whose necessities lead him to achieve with his life some tangible result, however mean. But look at the unfortunates among us, who are weighed down by the load of inherited gold below the necessity of exercising any intellectual power. Every young millionaire is not a genius, thank Heaven; and a commonplace rich man: how infinitely less are his chances than a commonplace poor man's!

Old Peter Grant worked hard and constantly in his South Street counting-room. That man must know little of him who should accuse the stanch old merchant of covetousness. He sought money, not for money's sake, but for occupation's sake. He put his whole soul into his work. If only the work were worth a soul! Only fools depreciate wealth. In our hearts says Emerson, "we honor the rich, because they have externally the freedom, power, and grace which we feel to be proper to man—proper to us." But our wants overlay our lives and outgrow any possible wealth; and so the man who once sought wealth as a means comes to strive for it as an end, and, O vain goose! lays his diurnal golden egg, and cackles in dismal contentment over the wretched performance. Is it a wonder that J. Augustus sinks the shop,

which, by the way, he has not raised, and takes not kindly to the paternal ways? The better instinct of youth re-
fuses to give up to this life, whose routine must crush out
all true enjoyment of existence. Show him an object to
gain with his money, and he will coin his brain and muscle into dollars unreluctant. But to begin where his father will leave off, and dutifully go on accumulating?
The bee is a very moral and prudent insect, praised of
Benjamin Franklin, and held in esteem by all lovers of
honey. But a young man is not a bee. Neither, O
man and father, is your son a duplicate Benjamin Franklin—bound in calf. Why try to make him swallow the
scandalous selfishness of Poor Richard? Can you not
see how infinitely more glorious was old Ben Franklin's
life than his shrewd, wretched maxims?

In the eyes of future generations, say of Lord Macaulay's philosophic New Zealander, that nation will be
counted greatest and wisest which has made the best use
of its rich young men. At present England is like to
carry off this prize; where, to an honest commonplace
rich man there is opened at least the door of Parliament
House. I hold that the man who is neither a fool nor a
genius, and who has a good competence, is he who is
most likely to serve the State with honor and profit.
But for such young fellows our customs provide nothing,
and they must go the ways of their fathers in South
Street, or, do worse! " Content to be merely the thriv-
ing merchants of a State, where they might be its guides,
counsellors, and rulers." Our theory calls for only men of
genius in the councils of the nation. And our practice

so fills them with the genius of blackguardism, that honest mediocrity reasonably fears to soil its fingers on the balustrades of the State Capitol.

So James Augustus tilted his chair against the club window, and soiled his hands neither in the Capitol nor in South Street.

The good fruit of utter indolence is that it awakens thought. A bright flicker precedes the final extinction of the lamp; and in the throes which, to the idler, shadow impending mental dissolution, the man sometimes finds out things. Generally a right thing—not always the right thing. To J. A., yawning and desperately musing amid the ruins of his Carthage, it was revealed that he did not love Maud Elbert. Had never loved her. Should never love her. That she did not love him. That he was not worthy of her. Why should they marry? Pondering which new view our young man finally came to the resolution that, though the thing was hardly the thing in him, and though probably Grant & Elbert would be displeased, yet he must tell Maud this.

You see it is possible that a young man shall be very idle without being hopelessly bad.

How to tell her? Your true epicure, who has tickled his palate with the best dishes of the most famous cooks, comes at last gladly back to plain bread and butter and tea; and J. A., having exhausted his imagination in devising schemes for conveying to Maud this new light of his, came at last to the sensible determination that a few honest words, spoken with at least the affectation of man-

K 2

liness, would best achieve the desired result. And thus it was done:

"You do not love me. I do not love you. Why should we two consider ourselves bound by the fond promises of our fathers? I love no one else, nor do you." If she had, perhaps the excellent Augustus would not have given her up so cheerfully; but let that pass. "Why live in this strait jacket? Let us cry quits, and at least feel honestly toward each other."

Maud opened her great blue eyes in silent surprise, and, as she took the young man's offered hand, cast upon him a more kindly look than he had ever received from her before. Evidently she had not thought it was in him; and he was too well pleased to have it all over to find fault with the dubious compliment. So these two ceased to be lovers but; became from that moment friends; a friendship which helped them to a better perception of life; for this light, which had so illuminated their former relation, also shed its faint gleam upon all other parts of their lives, and gave them a clearer insight into the power and use of those mysteries which we call circumstances. They stood upon new ground; and, insensibly, their attitude to the world was changed.

Not that the change was very perceptible, even to themselves. J. A. still tilted his chair back and smoked his cigar, and, for all I know, this one honest deed done, was fast returning to his spew, when— Have you ever observed how fatal it is to a prosperous fool to do one sensible act, to a successful rogue to be in one instance honest? This marks a point in his career; Fate pursues him remorselessly; will not let him stand still on this middle ground; says to him, "Backward or forward: here is no rest for you." Providence seems to acknowledge no good deed which stands alone; and, as in the boy's game of prisoner's base, the unlucky venturer on new ground finds himself chased on both sides, and has no peace till he elects his future.

When the panic of 1857 came on, no house stood firmer than Grant & Elbert. Their paper was gilt-edged in the banks; their credit was without a shadow; their business was, though widely extended, really prosperous. But two India clippers, uninsured, that should have come safely home were lost by the way; others lay rotting, freightless, in foreign ports; houses in whose stability they were vitally interested, one after another went to the ground; and one morning it was announced that Grant & Elbert were down—hopelessly down.

Old Grant sat silent, like a stern old Roman, in the deserted counting-room, and wound up affairs, which, alas! should never go again; wound up as fast as things could be wound up in those crazy times when Wall Street was financially insane as well as insolvent, and all the world was mad with fright. Sacrificed every dollar, every cent, to give each creditor his due—needlessly, some said, for scarce any one would do the like for him; but not needlessly, said stanch old Peter, when his honest fame and fair mercantile character were at stake. And every man was paid one hundred cents in the dollar; and Grant & Elbert were beggared. When all the clerks and retainers of the house had received their sal-

aries in full, and a moderate gift to help them through
the hard times; when all claims were adjusted, all goods
sacrificed; when the rusty, honest old sign was taken
down, and Grant & Elbert was a firm no longer, then old
Peter, looking prouder than in his best days—if these indeed were not his best days—began to turn about for a
shelter from the remainder of the great storm. His
house and Elbert's had been put into the general settle-
ment, and the families were now but tenants by courtesy
in Fifth Avenue. Now it was conveniently remembered
that, in a quiet village a few miles out of town, Maud
Elbert owned, in her own right, a humble cottage with
some ground attached—so humble, indeed, that it had
scarce ever had a moment's thought from her, except
when she remembered that here her father was born.

Hither George Elbert and Peter Grant removed; here
to await in quiet, and what peace they might, the clearing up of the financial atmosphere. Here Maud received them, having gone up some days in advance, with
a faithful old servant and what little resources had been
saved from the great wreck, to prepare their new home
for the old men. Here, she—worthy, thrice worthy the
high fate which had now befallen her—served them, as
who could do so well, with cheery smile and brightening
eye, like a very queen in her palace; remembering all
their old accustomed ways, and hours, and whims; ca-
tering frugally to all their simple old tastes; putting her
fair hands to all work from bread-making to bed-making;
and accomplishing all with the air of one born to do just
this. As was she not? Here dawned her happiest

hours; and here, too, the old merchants basked in her sunshine till they forgot their toils and troubles, their weary struggles and sore disappointments, and were fain to acknowledge, though faintly, and by no means too assuredly, that in all their magnificence they had known no such happiness and comfort as here.

And J. A.? In the general upsetting and remodelling of things, poor, useless, cigar-smoking J. A. had been totally forgotten. When the sea is calm, and the wind fair, the idlers of a ship make more noise and show than the oldest salt on board, and old Sheet-anchor Jack, who in such times seems rather a fifth wheel to this fast-rolling coach, and a useless piece of lumber, must be content to chew his cud of sweet and bitter fancies in silent waiting, under lee of the long-boat. But when the gale, which no one thought could by any possibility overtake so fast and stanch a clipper, does break its fury over her, then Sheet-anchor Jack comes out of his hole, and quietly makes all snug, while your boasting braggart idler is not even of sufficient value to pull and haul. So J. A., who had hitherto enacted the part of chief butterfly so much to his own admiration, now slunk wretchedly into his hole, and was content to be forgotten. Content?

Of course he was included in the general ruin; was shorn of his gay colors, divested of his trotting pony, his tailor, his fine society, his club. Last, unkindest cut of all—to give up his club! To hear him groan, you would have thought him a very Hercules, disarmed with not half his labors accomplished. The dear club! which got along quite as well without him as with him.

Though, to be sure, when you consider what a potent weapon it had been in his hands against his arch-fiend and enemy—ennui, it is not so surprising that he cherished its memory.

He had not lived at home for some time before the final catastrophe. Our young men, knowing the discomfort their inanities and idlings must cause. their simple parents, take care to leave home as soon as they are half fledged, and in the enjoyment of a preposterous allowance, or an opening in South Street. When J. A.'s salary ceased to be paid, he found it prudent to come home to dinner, where he sat with solemn and helpless visage, bolting his hasty food, and retiring to his den up stairs immediately after. I don't know whether he or his father most keenly appreciated his abject helplessness; but I think J. A., who was, after all, merely useless, and not altogether graceless, was touched by the old man's silent grieved glance, and reticence of just scorn ; remembering that now, when he might gladly be a support to the "governor," he was only a clog. As for old Peter, I dare say that now, when he could no longer indulge his boy, he saw that he should sooner have trained him.

It was Maud who first mentioned the illustrious name of James Augustus in their new home in the country. Old Peter looked up sternly at this mention, and bade her give herself no thought about so useless a lout; and for a time, apparently, she obeyed. Meanwhile J. A., feeling that he must somehow look out for himself, embarked in this new enterprise with, it must be said, some little misgivings as to the result. Things, financially speaking, were yet in such a state of general upsetness that old friends of Grant & Elbert, who might otherwise have given the young man a trial, were obliged to say, " Wait till times clear up." Pending which clearing up, Master J. A., I suspect, found some difficulties attending the management of the commissariat department, and was forced to make occasional little calls upon an accommodating uncle, trading at the sign of three gilt balls, whose business, happily, had not suffered in the general depression, and who was able, therefore, to make the youth small cash advances upon certain superfluous articles of jewelry, and a chronometer which was no longer needed to time fast horses on the Bloomingdale Road.

If idleness, as we have seen, is a partial illuminator of the dull mind, I am sure the breadless condition is the source of much greater light. There is such intimate connection between the stomach and the brain, that, as a full dinner temporarily disables your most acute thinker, so given a certain vacuum in the region of the digestive organs, and you have almost invariably a singularly lucid brain. So in J. A.'s needy condition he was as one blind from whose eyes the scales had suddenly fallen. Not one thing, but many, did he find out; and though at first "he saw men as trees walking," presently these new lights took order in his brain, and he discerned his course more clearly before him. But the question of bread was the most potent and imminent.

He had caused it to be generally known that a bookkeeper's place, even at a very moderate salary, would be temporarily acceptable to him; but he discovered that many other and abler applicants were before him here; that even a poor entry-clerk's situation might be a dozen times filled in as many minutes; and finally, pressed by circumstances, and slowly gathering courage to look Fortune in the face, which is the only way successfully to advance upon that fickle jade, he was content to accept of a porter's situation in the store of an honest but not overcourteous Quaker, who advised him to "sink Fifth Avenue, and turn to his work like a man." Five dollars per week made him happy for the time—a happiness which was dimmed by the jeers of his fellow-porters at his lack of muscle and his awkwardness. In his prosperity he had foolishly looked down upon these rough, strong men; now, how he envied them their brawn and their knack.

It was no small step gained for J. A. when he found pride in his work, in his increasing skill and muscle, and ceased to take thought for his soft hands. One day it was revealed to him that a man might be porter and gentleman too—if only he have his heart in the right place. "Whatsoever thy hand findeth to do, do it with thy might." It was not Poor Richard who said that. And now to J. A. came a singular and novel doubt of his own capacities and true value, a promising sign, truly; for this doubt was to him the beginning of all wisdom. He who had so valiantly applied for a book-keeper's place found it expedient to study somewhat of that intricate mercantile science. So to this he devoted his evenings, now relieved of that stress of invitations which formerly gave him his knowledge of books chiefly from their outsides and titles. By the flickering gas-light he patiently explored the abstruse and cabalistic Dr. and Cr., Ledger, Day-book, Journal, Cash-book; and having mastered this one thing, found he had conquered himself. It is not a bad thing to have been richly born and daintily nurtured. Let no man despise it. No soul that has ever come from heaven but longs to get back, and in this longing conceives and treasures the very idea of immortality and God. To poor J. A., dimly seeing his to-be, the past was now a landmark enabling him more definitely to lay out that future which should be the goal of his regenerate ambition and his honest toils.

With what secret joy did he indite a letter to old Peter, telling him modestly his present deeds, and hinting to him what he dared of his hopes! With what pride the old man read the letter aloud; his eyes filling, and his old voice trembling as he felt the new spirit of his boy! Maud's dear eyes flashed out a bright comprehension of the whole change; and old Elbert proposed at once to have J. A. up to the house. To which Peter wisely demurred, preferring that the boy's new career should not be interrupted by untimely temptation of praise.

There are so few honest and punctual men in the world that one who has these qualities needs to be very stupid indeed not to gain his step on the ladder, if only he has also the gift of patience. So it happened that J. A.'s employer presently discovered him to be of too great value for a mere porter, one needing chiefly muscle and a moderate degree of temperance, and ere the summer was over which followed the great panic, Peter's boy was assistant book-keeper. And now, at last, he could look his father in the face. So one Saturday afternoon, gaining an early leave for the purpose, he sailed up to the village where Maud's house gave the old man shelter. A sad breaking down, indeed, his old associates would have thought could they have seen him for one hesitating moment at the gate. Poor fellow! no longer mincing in his gait; no longer nattily gloved in daintiest kid; no longer adorned in coat and hat of latest style and finest make; but truly a man—standing firmly upon his feet, as one who possesses his soul in wholesome content; and looking you clearly in the eye, with a consciousness of honorable toil-won bread; not haughty or supercilious; but humbly proud, as one who has learned the great lesson of obedience, and knows that to obey is truly to command.

So they met—the old man and his son. I am not so base as to attempt for you a sketch of this sacred scene; if you can not feel it in your heart, I am not fit to tell it. Peter felt the blood of twenty years ago coursing through his veins, and George Elbert almost swore for extreme joy to see the boy come home. And Maud?

Sweet Maud! her life had blossomed here, indeed, and borne such fruit of joy to these old men, of peace and uttermost content, that their every breath asked blessings upon her dear head—their every thought was a prayer for her happiness. A very queen, indeed, as is every true woman in the home where she reigns supreme in love and good works; counting no labor drudgery which gives her loved ones comfort. What is drudgery indeed? Only that work which masters the worker. To the true heart no toil which is necessary to give peace and good cheer to any loved soul is mean or commonplace. Such a one no labor can master. To such no toil is drudgery.

Why should I not tell it? There was still one thing to be found out; and this revelation was to be made to both Maud and J. A. They are to be married in September. J. A. has but an assistant book-keeper's modest salary: I am sorry I stand in his way to speedy promotion. But his wife will bring him good health, and a brave kind heart as ever beat. When J. A., the other day, under pretense of finding something in my ledger, asked me to stand up with him, he said he "thought they should be happy."

I shouldn't wonder; for my wife says theirs is really a Love Match.

It is a work of real historical value, the result of accurate criticism, written in a liberal spirit, and from first to last deeply interesting.—*Athenæum.*

The style is excellent, clear, vivid, eloquent; and the industry with which original sources have been investigated, and through which new light has been shed over perplexed incidents and characters, entitles Mr. Motley to a high rank in the literature of an age peculiarly rich in history.—*North British Review.*

It abounds in new information, and, as a first work, commands a very cordial recognition, not merely of the promise it gives, but of the extent and importance of the labor actually performed on it.—*London Examiner.*

Mr. Motley's "History" is a work of which any country might be proud.—*Press* (London).

Mr. Motley's History will be a standard book of reference in historical literature.—*London Literary Gazette.*

Mr. Motley has searched the whole range of historical documents necessary to the composition of his work.—*London Leader.*

This is really a great work. It belongs to the class of books in which we range our Grotes, Milmans, Merivales, and Macaulays, as the glories of English literature in the department of history. * * * Mr. Motley's gifts as a historical writer are among the highest and rarest.—*Nonconformist* (London).

Mr. Motley's volumes will well repay perusal. * * * For his learning, his liberal tone, and his generous enthusiasm, we heartily commend him, and bid him good speed for the remainer of his interesting and heroic narrative.—*Saturday Review.*

The story is a noble one, and is worthily treated. * * * Mr. Motley has had the patience to unravel, with unfailing perseverance, the thousand intricate plots of the adversaries of the Prince of Orange; but the details and the literal extracts which he has derived from original documents, and transferred to his pages, give a truthful color and a picturesque effect, which are especially charming.—*London Daily News.*

M. Lothrop Motley dans son magnifique tableau de la formation de notre République.—G. GROEN VAN PRINSTERER.

Our accomplished countryman, Mr. J. Lothrop Motley, who, during the last five years, for the better prosecution of his labors, has established his residence in the neighborhood of the scenes of his narrative. No one acquainted with the fine powers of mind possessed by this scholar, and the earnestness with which he has devoted himself to the task, can doubt that he will do full justice to his important but difficult subject.—W. H. PRESCOTT.

The production of such a work as this astonishes, while it gratifies the pride of the American reader.—*N. Y. Observer.*

The "Rise of the Dutch Republic" at once, and by acclamation, takes its place by the "Decline and Fall of the Roman Empire," as a work which, whether for research, substance, or style, will never be superseded.—*N. Y. Albion.*

A work upon which all who read the English language may congratulate themselves.—*New Yorker Handels Zeitung.*

Mr. Motley's place is now (alluding to this book) with Hallam and Lord Mahon, Alison and Macaulay in the Old Country, and with Washington Irving, Prescott, and Bancroft in this.—*N. Y. Times.*

THE authority, in the English tongue, for the history of the period and people to which it refers.—*N. Y. Courier and Enquirer.*

This work at once places the author on the list of American historians which has been so signally illustrated by the names of Irving, Prescott, Bancroft, and Hildreth.—*Boston Times.*

The work is a noble one, and a most desirable acquisition to our historical literature.—*Mobile Advertiser.*

Such a work is an honor to its author, to his country, and to the age in which it was written.—*Ohio Farmer.*

Published by HARPER & BROTHERS,

Franklin Square, New York.

HARPER & BROTHERS will send the above Work by Mail (postage paid (for any distance in the United States under 3000 miles), on receipt of the Money.

History of
The United Netherlands.

FROM THE DEATH OF WILLIAM THE SILENT TO THE TWELVE YEARS' TRUCE.
WITH A FULL VIEW OF THE ENGLISH-DUTCH STRUGGLE AGAINST
- SPAIN, AND OF THE ORIGIN AND DESTRUCTION
OF THE SPANISH ARMADA.

BY JOHN LOTHROP MOTLEY, LL.D., D.C.L.,

Corresponding Member of the Institute of France, Author of "The Rise of the
Dutch Republic."

With Portraits and Map.

4 vols. 8vo, Muslin, $14 00.

Critical Notices.

His living and truthful picture of events.—*Quarterly Review* (London), Jan.,
1861.

Fertile as the present age has been in historical works of the highest merit,
none of them can be ranked above these volumes in the grand qualities of interest,
accuracy, and truth.—*Edinburgh Quarterly Review*, Jan., 1861.

This noble work.—*Westminster Review* (London).

One of the most fascinating as well as important histories of the century.—*Cor.
N. Y. Evening Post.*

The careful study of these volumes will infallibly afford a feast both rich and
rare.—*Baltimore Republican.*

Already takes a rank among standard works of history.—*London Critic.*

Mr. Motley's prose epic.—*London Spectator.*

Its pages are pregnant with instruction.—*London Literary Gazette.*

We may profit by almost every page of his narrative. All the topics which agi-
tate us now are more or less vividly presented in the History of the United Netherlands.—*New York Times.*

Bears on every page marks of the same vigorous mind that produced "The Rise
of the Dutch Republic;" but the new work is riper, mellower, and though equally
racy of the soil, softer flavored. The inspiring idea which breathes through Mr.
Motley's histories and colors the whole texture of his narrative, is the grandeur of
that memorable struggle in the 16th century by which the human mind broke the
thraldom of religious intolerance and achieved its independence.—*The World, N. Y.*

The name of Motley now stands in the very front rank of living historians. His
Dutch Republic took the world by surprise; but the favorable verdict then given
is now only the more deliberately confirmed on the publication of the continued
story under the title of the *History of the United Netherlands.* All the nerve,
and power, and substance of juicy life are there, lending a charm to every page.—
Church Journal, N. Y.

Motley, indeed, has produced a prose epic, and his fighting scenes are as real,
spirited, and life-like as the combats in the Iliad.—*The Press* (Phila.).

His history is as interesting as a romance, and as reliable as a proposition of Euclid. Clio never had a more faithful disciple. We advise every reader whose
means will permit to become the owner of these fascinating volumes, assuring him
that he will never regret the investment.—*Christian Intelligencer, N. Y.*

Published by HARPER & BROTHERS,
Franklin Square, New York.

☞ HARPER & BROTHERS will send the above Work by Mail, postage pre-paid
for any distance in the United States under 3000 miles), on receipt of the Money.

By George Eliot.

ADAM BEDE. 12mo, Cloth, $1 50.

FELIX HOLT, THE RADICAL. 8vo, Paper, 75 cents.
A Library Edition, 12mo, Cloth, $1 75.

THE MILL ON THE FLOSS. 12mo, Cloth, $1 50; 8vo, Paper,
75 cents.

ROMOLA. With Illustrations. 8vo, Cloth, $2 00; Paper, $1 50.

SCENES OF CLERICAL LIFE. 8vo, Paper, 75 cents.

SILAS MARNER, THE WEAVER OF RAVELOE. 12mo, Cloth,
$1 50.

It was once said of a very charming and high-minded woman that to know her was in itself a liberal education; and we are inclined to set an almost equally high value on an acquaintance with the writings of "George Eliot." For those who read them aright they possess the faculty of educating in its highest sense, of invigorating the intellect, giving a healthy tone to the taste, appealing to the nobler feelings of the heart, training its impulses aright, and awakening or developing in every mind the consciousness of a craving for something higher than the pleasures and rewards of that life which only the senses realize, the belief in a destiny of a nobler nature than can be grasped by experience or demonstrated by argument. On those readers who are able to appreciate a lofty independence of thought, a rare nobility of feeling, and an exquisite sympathy with the joys and sorrows of human nature, "George Eliot's" writings can not fail to exert an invigorating and purifying influence, the good effects of which leaves behind it a lasting impression.—*London Review.*

"George Eliot," or whoever he or she may be, has a wonderful power in giving an air of intense reality to whatever scene is presented, whatever character is portrayed.—*Worcester Palladium.*

She resembles Shakspeare in her power of delineation. It is from this characteristic action on the part of each of the members of the *dramatis personæ* that we feel not only an interest, even and consistent throughout, but also an admiration for "George Eliot" above all other writers.—*Philadelphia Evening Telegraph.*

Few women—no living woman indeed—have so much strength as "George Eliot," and, more than that, she never allows it to degenerate into coarseness. With all her so-called "masculine" vigor, she has a feminine tenderness, which is nowhere shown more plainly than in her descriptions of children.—*Boston Transcript.*

She looks out upon the world with the most entire enjoyment of all the good that there is in it to enjoy, and with an enlarged compassion for all the ill that there is in it to pity. But she never either whimpers over the sorrowful lot of man, or snarls and chuckles over his follies and littlenesses and impotence.—*Saturday Review.*

Her acquaintance with different phases of outward life, and the power of analyzing feeling and the working of the mind, are alike wonderful.—*Reader.*

"George Eliot's" novels belong to the enduring literature of our country—durable, not for the fashionableness of its pattern, but for the texture of its stuff.—*Examiner.*

PUBLISHED BY HARPER & BROTHERS, NEW YORK.

HARPER & BROTHERS *will send any of the above works by Mail, postage prepaid, to any part of the United States, on receipt of the price.*

www.ingramcontent.com/pod-product-compliance
Lightning Source LLC
Chambersburg PA
CBHW020111030726

47498CB00006B/2054